Puffin Books

Legions of the Eagle

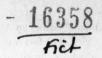

An Introduction by the Author

This is the story of a boy who lived at the time of the first real
Roman invasion of Britain, and it is written for the pleasure of
boys and girls between the ages of nine and twelve.

Julius Caesar had visited this island twice before, but largely as a
means of obtaining information about it. However, in A.D. 43 the
Emperor Claudius sent his general, Aulus Plautius, to do the job
properly! Now, the British peoples with whom Aulus Plautius
had the most trouble were the Belgae, a warlike group of tribes
who had only recently come from Gaul themselves, and so
already knew something of Roman methods. The boy-hero of this
tale, Gwydion, is one of these Belgae. His father is a farmer near
Colchester, though when he is needed he forms one of the
war-band of the young Belgic king, Caratacus.

The Romans broke the strength of these Belgae near Colchester,
using those strange animals, the elephants, as a means of
terrifying the native charioteers. After this, Caratacus fled to what
is now South Wales, and soon became ruler over the people there.
He continued to give the Romans a great deal of trouble until,
with the help of a British queen, Cartismandua, they captured
him and sent him to Rome. There his proud bearing was such
that the Emperor Claudius pardoned him and even allowed him
to live out his days peacefully as a pensioner.

It should be said that many peoples had been coming to Britain
since the dawn of history, and that they were each rather different
in race and outlook. Some were small and dark, some sturdy and
brown-haired, some red-haired, and some tall and fair-haired.
They were as different from each other as a present-day Swede

might be from an Arab. Yet we know them all by the name of Celts! The fact is that we class them according to the language which we think they spoke, Celtic; and this is represented in modern times by Irish Gaelic, Scots Gaelic, and Welsh. In Gwydion's time this language would be spoken over the greater part of Europe, and even understood as far as the borders of the country we now call Greece.

This is a story of battle and treachery, as might be expected where so many peoples were living together, each with its own kings and heroes and beliefs. But at the end you will see that the point the tale tries to make is that it doesn't matter what colour your hair is, or what language you speak. The important thing is – what sort of person are you?

If you feel that you need to, turn to pages 189 and 190. Some words that might be new to you are explained there. Though actually they don't matter, as long as you enjoy the story!

Henry Treece

Henry Treece

Legions of the Eagle

Illustrated by Christine Price

Puffin Books
in association with The Bodley Head

PUFFIN BOOKS

Published by the Penguin Group
27 Wrights Lane, London W8 5TZ, England
Viking Penguin Inc., 40 West 23rd Street, New York, New York 10010, USA
Penguin Books Australia Ltd, Ringwood, Victoria, Australia
Penguin Books Canada Ltd, 2801 John Street, Markham, Ontario, Canada L3R 1B4
Penguin Books (NZ) Ltd, 182–190 Wairau Road, Auckland 10, New Zealand

Penguin Books Ltd, Registered Offices: Harmondsworth, Middlesex, England

First published by The Bodley Head 1954
Published in Puffin Books 1965
20 19 18 17 16 15 14 13 12 11

Made and printed in Great Britain by
BPCC Hazell Books Ltd
Member of BPCC Ltd
Aylesbury, Bucks, England
Set in Linotype Baskerville

Contents

Part Four

PICTS

PICTS

BRIGANTES

HIBERNIA

BRIGANTES

River Abus

MONA

ORDOVICES

Vricon

ICENI

TRINOBANTES

BELGAE

Camulodunum

SILURIA

Londinium

ATREBATES CANTII

Sorbiodunum

DUROTRIGES

Mai Dun

VECTIS

Gesoriacum

ATREBATES BELGICA

To Lugdunum

GAUL

ARMORICA

VENETI

W   E

BRITAIN
IN
GWYDION'S
TIME

Showing
TRIBES
Forests
Marshes

S

Part One - AD 43

1 · A Knife for a Hare

It was high summer and young Gwydion of the Belgae
ran excitedly among the trees, his dog at his heels, hunting. Gwydion, who was almost thirteen, and a big boy
for his age, was the only son of Caswallawn, a lord who
rode at the right hand of Caratacus the king, so the boy's
dress, even when hunting, was rich and colourful, as
befitted his father's rank.

A fine sight he made, as he ran among the oak and the
hornbeam, on the green slopes above the city of Camulodunum. His long fair hair swept behind him in the
afternoon breeze, and his heavy linen cloak, coloured
red and blue and green to show which tribe he belonged
to, swung out behind him, held to his shoulders by
round bronze brooches with brightly enamelled centre-
pieces. He wore a tunic of thin deerskin, supple and
pliable, its edges sewn with silver thread; a broad red
belt about his middle, and light, fawn doeskin shoes on
his feet.

The dog which trotted behind him was of the greyhound type, but smaller and shaggier. He wore a narrow bronze collar round his neck, inscribed with
Gwydion's tribal sign.

So the two ran through the late afternoon of summer,
the sun's rays glinting on them both, lighting up the
dog's metal collar and the polished gold neck-ring and

shoulder-brooches of the boy. Together they made a
fine pair; yet such a pair as might have been seen almost anywhere in southern Britain at this time, for the
Belgae were powerful and rich, and had the secret of
working metals and of weaving fine cloth. Moreover,
they were a people who loved finery almost as much as
they adored battle, and that was a great deal!

At last the boy stopped and sat down, breathless. 'It's
no use, Bel,' he said. 'We shall never run down a deer
today! We are too fat and well-fed, my friend! Let us
call through the woods and see if Math has been lucky!'

Bel, the hound, seemed to understand his young master's words, and rose again, wagging his long tail at the
mention of Math's name.

'Math! Math! Where are you?' called Gwydion, his
hands to his mouth to make the sound carry through
the dense woodland. Bel began to bark at the echoes
that came back to them, eerie and startling from the
dark shadows of the wood where the sun never pene-
trated.

They waited for a while, and then Gwydion shrugged
and began to walk towards his father's house, which he
could just see, set high on a terraced hill, perhaps a mile
away.

But before he had gone far, the sound of shuffling
footsteps could be heard from the dim wood, and in a
few moments another boy stumbled out into the sunlight, gasping for breath and looking afraid.

'Where on earth have you been, Math?' asked Gwydion, a little cross from waiting. 'I bet you're the only
slave in these parts who is allowed to go running off like

that, on his own, and keeping his master's son waiting, as you have kept me!'

Math, who was a little older than Gwydion, and very dark-haired, gave a little salute, as though apologizing, and then began to gasp again. He was dressed in a simple linen tunic, with a raw-hide belt, and light running shoes of cowskin. He wore no jewellery, but was clean and obviously well cared for. Gwydion smiled when he saluted, for that small gesture satisfied the boy's pride, and now he was quite friendly to Math again.

'You must be in a terrible state, Math,' he said, kindly, 'when you forget to give me my proper due! And where are your bow and arrows? Have you lost them?'

Math looked at his companion with wide brown eyes and an expression of fear on his swarthy face. 'I flung them away,' he said hoarsely, almost as though he did not wish anyone to hear his words.

Gwydion stared at him in surprise. 'Flung them away!' he repeated. 'But, Math, how could you; my father brought you that bow all the way from Londinium. It was a Scythian bow, made of many strips of horn, not like an ordinary wooden bow. It cost him quite a lot of money, you know. Why, I'd have liked it myself. Why did you throw it away? Can I have it if I find it?'

Math fell on his knees before his friend. 'You must never touch it, Gwydion,' he said. 'It is taboo now. I had to fling it away.'

Gwydion looked down at him in consternation.

'What have you done, Math?' he said in a whisper. 'Have you killed a man?' Gwydion knew that though a free man could kill an opponent and even be praised for it, a slave had no right to take human life, not even in his own defence.

Math began to weep as he crouched among the grass. Then he looked up and gazed at Gwydion with terrified eyes. 'I have done worse than that,' he said. 'I have killed a – hare.'

His friend gave a small gasp of astonishment and for a moment seemed to draw away from him. Then he said, 'But, Math, that is a sacred animal; only *they* may kill it.' He did not name the druids as the only men who might kill the creature; he was afraid that they might hear him, in their strange, magic way, if he did, and know what Math had done straightway; and Gwydion was afraid of the druids, although one of his kindest uncles happened to be a druid.

'It wouldn't be quite so bad,' Gwydion went on, 'if the hare were not our own animal, yours and mine; the animal of our Brotherhood, the Brotherhood of the month we were born in, the two of us.'

Math dropped his head in his hands and wept without shame. 'Something dreadful is bound to happen, now, Gwydion,' he said. 'The gods are certain to punish me. I feel sure of it! Oh, what shall I do?'

Gwydion went to him and helped him up, putting his arm round him and trying to sound brave. 'The worst cannot happen,' he said, 'for your hair is black, and they, the holy ones, only sacrifice red-haired ones under the great Midsummer Stones. So it won't be that. Besides, an idea has struck me – you have no rights in law. In fact, as far as the law of the Belgae goes, you don't exist, for you are a slave.'

Math was a dark-skinned Silurian from the far west, who had been captured when he was a small boy, on some foraging raid that Gwydion's father had made. Therefore he did not come under Belgic law, which was laid down in the Council Chamber of Caratacus in Camulodunum. Math listened, but his face was still clouded.

'That is all right for the law of men,' he said. 'But the gods have their own laws, and it is one of these I have broken. They do not care for the laws the Belgae make. The gods are their own law-makers.'

Gwydion looked uncertain for a moment, and bit his lip, as though in deep thought. At last he half-turned from Math and said, 'My father is responsible for you, both to the king and to the gods. But my father was not with us today and did not know what you were doing. He cannot be held responsible for something which he did not know about. So, I must be responsible, for I am my father's only son. Yes, I am responsible.'

Math tried to dissuade him from this point of view, but Gwydion shook him off, almost roughly, and his face was stern.

'If I were to make a sacrifice,' he said, 'the evil might pass away from our house. But for a hare it must be a sacrifice that causes me great suffering. I must give something to the gods that will cause me sorrow when I part with it.'

He looked to the ground and gave a deep sigh. Then,

without speaking to Math, he bent and began to stroke the head of Bel, the hound, who all this time had been looking at the two boys with great loving eyes, for they both cared for him and took him hunting almost every day. Then, as though he had made his mind up, Gwydion took Bel by the collar and turned with him towards the wood.

'Come on, Bel, old friend,' he said. 'I am sorry that it has come to this, but I will try to do it as painlessly as I can. You must lie still and I will be quick.'

When they were at the edge of the wood, Math could stand it no longer. He ran after them, 'Stop! Stop!' he cried. 'I would rather lie under the great stones myself than have Bel killed. Look, Gwydion, there is your fine hunting-knife. It cost more than Bel, and it has such a lovely red garnet-stone set into the hilt. I know you love it dearly, and it will be a great loss to you, but could you not give that to the gods, and spare Bel?'

A smile spread over Gwydion's face. 'Oh, Math,' he said, 'what a fool I was not to have thought of that before! Of course, it shall be the knife. I shall miss it terribly, and no doubt father will beat me for losing it, but we shall have Bel, shan't we!'

He loosed the dog, which ran to Math and jumped up at his chest in fun, almost as though he knew that the slave had saved him. Then Gwydion drew the bright knife, and swinging it out as far as his arm would go, he flung it in a glittering arc over the topmost boughs of the wood. They saw it glint in the last rays of the sun, and then they heard it strike a mass of foliage and tinkle down, somewhere distant, out of sight.

'Good luck go with you and come back to us,' said Gwydion, making the usual remark of Celtic boys who sacrificed a treasured belonging.

The boys looked at each other, and seemed to sigh with relief. Then they brightened up, and Gwydion even said, 'Well, the old gods shouldn't take it amiss, after all. One hare in exchange for a lovely bow and a better knife than the Roman Emperor carries, I'll bet!'

Math frowned a little, for he knew that one should not make slighting remarks concerning the gods. Then they linked arms and almost ran together towards the house on the hill, for they were hungry.

They skirted the terraced fields, which were set up the hillside and which carried a good yield of grain, knee-high russet corn-ears and oats; and they passed the outbuildings of the farm, where the plough and harrows were stored, and the chariot house, where Gwydion's father kept the great war-chariot that had been in the family since the time the Romans first came, led by Julius Caesar – or 'The Hairy One', as the Belgae used to call him, as they laughed about their fires at night.

And so on, until they came to the farm-house itself; a long, single-storeyed thatched building, with the stables at one end, and the sleeping-quarters at the other.

As they paused at the door to unlink their arms, for it was not considered correct for a freeman, like Gwydion, to behave in such a friendly manner towards a slave, Gwydion said, 'Math, we mustn't say a word about this to anyone. If father wants to know where my knife is, I shall say it is lost. That is not a lie, is it? After all, it *is* lost! I shall never find it again!'

Math said, 'Your parents have always been as kind as my own father and mother were, when they were alive. I do not like to deceive them.'

Gwydion said, 'Well, am I not kind to you as well! After all, you killed the hare, not me!'

'Very well,' said Math, his face darkening again as he recalled what he had done. 'I will not say anything.'

'No, not even if father beats me for losing it,' stressed Gwydion; and the two boys went into the great hall and sat down at the long oaken table and began to beat on the wood with their knives and bowls, as though indicating to the servants that they were extremely hungry and must be served without delay. But the two old waiting-women did not hurry when they heard this clatter, for the boys always did this, whether they were really hungry or not. So this day of all days they were made to wait as long as ever, while the oat-cakes were heated and the fresh milk skimmed for them.

2 · Shall It Be War?

Gwydion's fears were unfounded. His father came back to the farm later than usual, and accompanied by a dirt-caked tribesman whose long riding cloak hung about him in tatters and whose iron armour showed signs of neglect in the rust that had begun to eat into it at the edges of the embossed breast-plate. Gwydion heard them coming and looked through the small window hole, then drew back excitedly.

'Father is with a man of the Cantii, Math,' he said. 'One of the iron-working folk from the south. They look very serious indeed. There must be trouble somewhere.'

Math said, 'Do you think it's the Romans again?' His voice was almost disinterested, as though he had heard of trouble from the Romans many times, without it ever happening; and also as though the Romans were not his enemies, but the enemies of the Belgae.

Gwydion said, 'If the Romans have landed, the Cantii would know as soon as anyone in Britain, and they would send to Caratacus for help.'

'Only if they were being defeated,' said Math, with a wry smile on his dark face. 'The Cantii are too proud to ask for help unless they are being beaten in battle. They wish for all the glory. They would not want to share their victory with any other tribe. This man comes with news of defeat, you mark my words, Gwydion.'

Gwydion was a little angry and said sharply, 'We Belgae, we folk from Belgica, whatever our tribal names now, must stick together. If we do that, we shall defeat any foe, either Roman or German. You are a Silurian from the West; you do not know our great family power.'

Math's dark eyes seemed to smile, as though he knew a great deal but did not wish to say what he knew. At last he said, half to himself, 'We, the Silures, have been in Britain for many, many years. We had been here for countless winters before the Belgae had even heard of Britain. We are an old people and know many things. And one thing we know is that Rome is powerful and cannot be defeated by a group of tribes who are each too proud to join together, unless they are facing defeat.'

Gwydion looked at him sternly. 'Did not our great ancestor Cassiveleaunus turn away Julius the Caesar?' he said with pride.

Math grinned and said, 'Julius came the first time merely to see what Britain was like. And the second time he simply wished to show what power Rome had, nothing more. Had he wished to stay here and conquer, he might have done so. But he had other, more important battles to fight in Gaul.'

Gwydion jumped from his bench and raised his hand as though he would strike the slave; but before he could do so, his mother came bustling in, and swept them out of the hall.

'Boys, boys,' she said, 'away with you! Play outside, for your father has important things to discuss with a visitor from far afield.'

Gwydion's mother was a kindly woman who made no distinction between the two boys, for she loved children whether they were slaves or not, and came from the peasant community of the Atrebates in the wooded middle of the country. She was a strongly made woman, fair-haired, and dressed in a serviceable woollen dress, with an apron and sleeves rolled back, for she liked to help her dairymaid, and to keep an eye on what went on in the big cool kitchen at the back of the house. The boys loved her and respected her at the same time, for,

as they both knew, she was usually too busy to tell a
lad twice to do things! The second command was often
accompanied by a good sound smack. They had both
felt the force of this argument, and so when she came
into the hall, they stopped bickering and went by the
back door outside into the broad, palisaded yard.

There, a new sight met their eyes; two grooms were
scrubbing down the war-chariot, cleaning it of its old
caked mud, and burnishing the bronze decorations
along the single shaft on which the archer stood when
the vehicle went into battle. The sword-smith was bending over the wheels, a rough stone in his hand, sharpening the long scythe-like blades that projected from the
axles on either side of the chariot.

He looked up as the boys approached, his tanned and
wrinkled face smiling grimly. 'Here's something you
lads have never seen before,' he said. 'These two knives
have not been sharpened in your time, I warrant!'

The boys stood back and watched him, stricken with
awe. The two knives looked terribly sharp already, and
yet the smith went on honing them, as though they were
blunt bars of iron.

At last Gwydion said, 'Is it the Romans, Dillus?'

The smith pursed his mouth and, shaking his head,
said, 'It's not my place to pass on rumours to young
lads. I only know what I do know, and that's all. Your
father told me to do this, and so I am doing it. Go and
ask him, if you want to know!'

He grinned at the boys, for he knew that Gwydion
would not dare to ask his father about anything as
serious as this. Then he went on working, and the two

lads whistled Bel and strolled off into the fields, hoping to start a rabbit from the gorse bushes that fringed the farm.

Yet, though they whistled and sang in a carefree manner, both of them were thinking the same thing: Were the gods about to bring misfortune on the family of Gwydion? And was that because Math had killed the sacred hare? They hid this thought from each other, but it ran in their minds all the same, until at last they returned and went to their beds.

Gwydion saw the bright torchlight still burning in the hall as he pulled the hide coverlets over him and tried to settle down on his mattress of springy heather and fern fronds. This worried him and he could not sleep, for the glow struck under the door of his cubicle. Moreover, he could hear the sound of armour being scrubbed and of a sword or a knife being rubbed rhythmically against a sharpening stone. He did not dare go into the hall to see what was happening, for his father was very strict about things like that. So he lay on his bed, too curious to sleep, and wishing that his father would say something from the other room that would give him an idea of what was going on; but all he heard at last was his father's voice, bidding his mother good night and telling her that a guard would be posted at the gate of the farm and that she was not to be afraid. Then he heard the hall door close, and his father calling to one of the grooms to bring him a horse and to see that the visitor's charger was well saddled.

Gwydion waited for a few minutes, then, acting on an impulse, he rose from his bed and tapped on the horse-hide partition that separated him from Math. There was no reply, and Gwydion did not dare risk shouting. He decided that Math must be fast asleep, and so decided that he must do what he wished to do alone.

He slipped on his tunic and trousers, and wrapped a wolf-skin about his shoulders, for the nights were chilly on the hills, and he did not want to catch a cold just at this moment of excitement.

Then, when all was quiet in the hall, Gwydion squeezed through the window-hole above his bed, ran the few yards to the stockade, and clambered up and over, falling lightly into the fern on the other side. Then, without turning to look back once, he set his course down the hill, in the direction his father's horse must have taken, towards the great royal city of Camulodunum.

He saw no one but an old shepherd as he raced over the undulating fields, and that old man was too frightened to do more than run into his little hut of clay and wattles, and pull the door to behind him. Then, running among the grazing sheep so silently that he hardly disturbed them, Gwydion came to the beaten earth pathway that led at last to the town gates.

As he approached the tall posterns, he saw in the moonlight that the sentries were on watch, holding their long spears at the ready. No doubt they would let him in, for they knew him quite well as his father was so important at the court; but this night they would surely escort him to his father, and that was just what Gwydion didn't want to happen. So he turned away from the town gates and skirted the wall for a few hundred yards,

until he came to a place where the coping had fallen
from the top and the wall was a little lower than at
other parts. He knew this place well, and fumbled in
the ditch until he found what he sought. It was a long
pole, a pine sapling that the other boys hid there for
those occasions when they were locked out of the town
at night and must return home or get a thrashing.

Gwydion stepped back for twenty paces, then ran
at the wall. Just before he reached the stones, he dug
his pole deep into the soft earth and leaped with all
his force. He sailed over the wall, leaving the sapling
upright in the ground.

Gwydion had done this many times successfully, but
this night his luck was out. Even as he was falling into
the citadel he saw below him in the bright moonlight,
a fat citizen, a butcher or a tanner – at least, a prosperous man, walking with a lady as plump as himself, and
a small boy. It was unavoidable. Gwydion crashed down,
almost on top of the man, and they both rolled over in
the roadway, gasping with the impact. Almost at once
the woman began to cry out that the enemy was enter-
ing the city, and the small boy raised his staff and began to beat Gwydion about the head, saying that he
would be revenged for his poor father. The poor father
lay so still for a while that Gwydion was afraid he had
killed him. Then the man began to stir and groan, and
Gwydion, wrapping the wolf-skin about his head so
that he would not be recognized, ran into a side-turning,
among the overhanging thatch roofs, and tried to get
his breath back before going on. However, soon he
heard a commotion and saw the lights of torches burn-

ing in the main street. He knew then that the woman's cries had aroused the guards, and so he could not wait any longer.

Keeping to the shadows of the low-built houses, he ran as fast as he could, and by the time he reached Caratacus's hall, the sounds of pursuit had faded away.

The hall was brightly lit and Gwydion could see that many lords must be there, for chariots and horses were waiting before the great doors, attended by grooms and men-at-arms. The boy moved round to the back of the tall wooden building, and, choosing his opportunity, ran into the dark shadow which it cast across the ground, and looked for a means of reaching a window that opened a few feet above his head.

As he stood there, hardly daring to breathe, he heard the sound of horns from inside the hall, and knew then that Caratacus the king was about to speak. He could not catch the words that were said, but he understood by their tone that the king was defiant, and he heard the great growl of applause that greeted them. Then he heard another voice, a voice which he knew only too well. He was too excited to think what he was doing, almost, but he felt that he must see inside the hall. He took a short run and leaped lightly up towards the window. His fingers grasped the ledge, and silently he pulled himself up until he could see into the room. There a sight met his eyes which he never forgot.

His father was striding up and down the long hall, his head thrown back and his arms waving as he spoke in a loud voice. Warriors on either side of him parted as he approached them, to give him free passage, and the king himself smiled down at him from his high chair set on a dais at the end of the room.

Gwydion suddenly felt his heart swell with pride for his father! What a soldier he looked, his long plaits swinging below the gold helmet, from the sides of which rose the fierce bull's horns; his arms blazing with light as the torches caught the many gold bracelets on his wrists; the gold gorget at his throat burning like a fire; his scarlet cloak thrown back over one shoulder to expose the burnished plates of his body armour! No wonder such a man was the favourite henchman of Caratacus!

Gwydion almost shouted with glee himself, as his father swore to beat the Romans back to Gaul with one hand tied behind his back! Everyone roared with laughter as Caswallawn gave an imitation of a Roman officer, mincing and prancing up and down the room. 'Is this the redoubtable Roman army?' he asked, among loud laughter. 'Why, *we* need not fight them! We could send our young sons to fight them!'

Then the mead horns were raised, and long toasts were drunk to Caratacus and Caswallawn, and the Belgae in general. In fact, as Gwydion hung there, above the ground, he thought they would never stop toasting each other, and he hoped that his father would return home sober when that war-meeting was finished.

Just then someone struck a chord on a harp, somewhere at the back of the room, and instantly the mead was forgotten and the warriors began to chant and to strike their swords against the boss of their metal shields. The noise was deafening, and its excitement swept

through Gwydion's heart like a shrill wind, until he almost fainted with the sheer thrill of seeing such great men making ready for war.

But just then another sound came to his ears. It was that of men running, and seeking someone, in haste and anxiety. Gwydion listened and distinguished the voices of the fat man whom he had knocked down earlier, and of his plump wife. They were on his trail, and the torch-light was approaching round the corner of the council hall. There was no time to waste; Gwydion slipped to the ground and ran swiftly to the front of the building, ducking under a chariot and stooping there, hardly breathing. He heard the sleepy groom of the chariot snoring, so he knew that he had not been seen. After a while there came the pattering of footsteps across the yard before the hall, and the torchlight flickered for an instant between the legs of horses and through the wheels of the chariots. Then Gwydion heard a guard begin to curse and tell the fat man that he must have been imagining things; and so at last they went away, and the boy breathed a sigh of relief. But now he was in a dilemma. He could not go back to the break in the wall, for there the guards would surely be waiting and he would be taken captive without a doubt. He thought for a moment, and then he pulled off the wolf-skin, by which he might have been recognized, and flung it into the shadows beneath the chariot. Then he stepped out into the open and walked purposefully through the town, towards the main gates.

No one questioned him. In fact, certain passers-by nodded or spoke to him, saying that it was a fine night, and wishing to be remembered to his mother when he got home.

At the gate it was a different matter, however, for the guards knew everyone who had entered the city that day, and they knew that Gwydion had not passed through their gates since morning. A Captain of Guard, a tall, broad-shouldered man with a scar across his cheek-bone that made him seem very frightening, slowly strode to meet the boy, his eyes stern, but his mouth half-smiling, under his drooping Celtic moustache.

'Halt!' he commanded, laying his hand on his long sword.

Gwydion smiled up at him. 'Certainly,' he said. 'What can I do for you, Captain?'

The soldier looked at first as though he might take hold of the boy and lay him across his knee; but in the end he smiled and said, 'So you must be the enemy who entered the city, young Gwydion?'

The boy looked surprised and said, 'What, me, Captain? I am no enemy, am I? Is it to fight me that my father has got his war-chariot all bright and polished today? I am surprised.'

The Captain turned to the sentry at the gate and said solemnly, 'Gwyn, take note of this boy. He is an enemy of the Belgae, in disguise, I shouldn't wonder! If ever you see him vaulting over the town wall at night again, you know what to do, don't you?'

The sentry put on a ferocious expression and drew his finger across his throat with a vicious hiss. Gwydion shuddered, for the man seemed to mean it! Then the

Captain gave him a push that sent him through the gates, and the sentry gave him a smack with the end of his spear that tingled for quite a time: and so Gwydion left Camulodunum for the last time for many years, after listening to the only war-council that he ever was to hear.

3 · The Man Under the Trees !

The journey back home was not a long one, but Gwydion did not feel that he wanted to return to his bed straightway. There was too much to think about; he was sure that he would never sleep if he went home immediately. So he turned away from the path, and took a route that led him out towards the woods where he and Math had been hunting earlier in the day.

Near the spot where he had stood to throw the knife in among the trees, Gwydion stopped and sat down on a flat stone, to think about the gallant scenes he had witnessed in the council chamber. He recalled the king, lolling in his carved oaken chair, a cow's horn full of mead in one hand and his other bejewelled hand caressing the head of his favourite greyhound which was always given a place beside the throne. He recalled his own father, strutting up and down, his face red with pride and wine, his words bold and brave, his arms making arcs of light in the torchlit hall as he swung them about, to emphasize his words. . . . Gwydion sighed with admiration for such things, for he was a true boy of the Belgae, a natural warrior, and he dreamed of the day when he would pass the initiation ceremonies and be allowed to ride with the king on a grey horse like the one his father rode. Then they would give him a battle-name, like 'War-Eagle', or 'Wolf', or, if his father was still living, they might call him 'Young Badger', for his father was 'The Badger'.

As Gwydion thought of this his heart was filled with pleasure, until he thought of Math, suddenly. Math could never be his friend then, for a lord could not ride with a mere slave. Gwydion's pride was stilled then and he half-turned towards the wood, his eyes a little moist, for he loved his friend, Math, as dearly as he loved Bel, and perhaps more. As he turned, his heart started up into his throat violently and he felt a great shudder run through his body. A man was sitting within the shadow of the wood, quite still, and watching him with bright, unwinking eyes.

Just then a shaft of moonlight struck inward through the foliage of the wood and Gwydion saw for an instant what the man looked like. His face was a dark brown, darker than Math's, and his eyes were as piercing as those of a hawk. His long nose was hooked and his lips curled in a cruel smile below the hanging moustaches that almost reached his chest. In his ears he wore dangling ornaments, and on his head towered a high conical hat of sheepskin, in which was stuck a heron's feather. His broad body was clothed with brightly coloured animal skins, held round the waist with a broad studded belt, into which was thrust a variety of knives such as the Belgic boy had never seen before. Yet what attracted Gwydion's attention more than anything else was the great bow which was slung over the stranger's shoulder. It was exactly like that which Math had flung away, but of course much longer and stronger. A wide sheaf of arrows lay across his knees, their feathered ends coloured red.

Gwydion saw all this in a flash, and then the moon withdrew her light, and Gwydion shook with fear as he heard the man moving towards him. At first, the boy was rooted to the spot, but as the man came out from the dark shadows, he was able to jump to his feet and begin to run in fear.

When he was twenty yards or more away from the wood, Gwydion looked back over his shoulder. The man had stopped at the edge of the wood and seemed to be laughing and calling something. Gwydion listened, but could not make out what it was. The language he was using was certainly not any sort of Celtic, nor was it Latin, for Gwydion had been to school in Camulodunum and had had a Roman teacher who had taught him from Caesar's book about the war in Gaul. This was something different, something the like of which he had never heard before.

Then a fearsome thought struck him. This must be a god of the woods, and the language he was speaking must be the language of the gods! Yes, that was it – this was a warning from the gods that Math, or Gwydion, or both, had done wrong! This god had come to punish them!

Gwydion began to run frantically towards the house on the hill; never looking back after that realization had come to him. Yet, when he was half-way there, he stopped, and another thought struck him. If this was a messenger of the gods, why hadn't he put an arrow to that great bow and shot it at Gwydion? Or, easier still, why had he not drawn one of those long knives and ... Gwydion shuddered at the awful thought. Then he became calmer. No, this god must be a kindly one. He must have come down to say that their guilt was forgiven, that their sacrifice of the bow and the knife had been sufficient to pay for the dead hare. Gwydion's mouth began to smile. He felt easier in his mind now and turned back, to look towards the wood. In the silver moonlight, he saw the man, but this time he was seated on a horse, a small shaggy pony rather than the sort of tall charger with which the boy was familiar; and he was waving something above his head. What was it? It looked like a creature of some sort. Yes, it was a hare, and he was waving it by the hind-feet, as though he were wishing Gwydion good-bye.

The boy's legs suddenly felt very weak, for he had been through much excitement since he had stolen from his bed that night. He began to make his way slowly to the house, still a little afraid, but now determined not to say a word about this strange encounter, lest the gods should be displeased a second time, and should take Bel from him.

4 · Death Looks in the Ditch!

The next morning, after a troubled night's sleep, Gwydion awoke to hear great bustling and commotion in the yard outside. He dressed quickly and went outside, to find the farm full of men and horses and stores. The great chariot was now bright and shining, and its blades and coral-studded harness all ready. The boy saw that the long trek-wagon had also been made ready and was now almost full of provisions and clothing. Among all the bustle of men arriving and departing on sweating horses, Gwydion saw his mother and father talking earnestly, in the thick of the people. When they saw him, they beckoned to him to come to them straightway. Then his father, who looked a little tired and red about the eyes, said, 'Gwydion boy, you will withdraw with your mother and the servants in the wagon, to a spot well away from the city. If all goes well, I shall ride to you tonight, or tomorrow night at the latest. If all goes badly, I shall try to get a messenger to bring you word that you are to retreat towards the west, into the wooded lands. Your mother knows which relatives we can trust out there, and she will be in charge if I do not return. Do you understand?'

Gwydion looked at him sadly and said, 'Father, can I be with you in the battle, if there is to be one?'

The father smiled and clapped his son on the shoulder. 'There is time for that later, Gwydion,' he said. 'For the moment, your task is to be a soldier of the wagon and guard your mother.'

Gwydion could see that there was no point in arguing, and he said, 'Will Math be with us?'

'Of course,' said his mother. 'We could not leave dear Math! Any more than we could leave you.' So Gwydion went away to eat his breakfast, and to tell the slave of the plan which they had to follow.

A little later, since there were still many preparations to be made, Gwydion went to his father and said, 'Father, it may be a long while before Math and I can go hunting with little Bel again. May we walk out among the hills for a while until the wagons are ready?'

The warrior smiled and said, 'You are a true hunter, my son. Nothing, not even battle, will stop you! Very well, but see that you run back when you hear three blasts on the war-horns, for they will mean that I shall set forth with the chariot to Camulodunum to meet the king, and that your mother's wagon will start out to the place which we have decided on. Do not delay or they will go without you; they must obey my orders.'

Gwydion bowed to his father and then called Math and Bel, and so they set off, to a warren that lay well to the south of the dark woods where Gwydion had seen the strange creature on the previous night.

As they walked, with Bel dancing at their heels, Gwydion breathed the summer air deeply and said, 'Oh, Math, it would be terrible to go away and never come back to my land again.'

But Math only smiled, a little sadly, and Gwydion didn't raise the topic again, for he suddenly remembered that this was what had already happened to poor Math. He held the slave's hand for a moment, as though assuring him that he was his friend, and then they went on. Soon Bel had smelled a rabbit and the two boys forgot their cares in digging frantically with their hands and with sticks, to try to find the hidden creature; but they were out of luck, and so passed on over the brow of the hill, that looked south almost towards Londinium itself. And there they paused and stood still in amazement, pointing and shading their eyes with their hands.

Far away across the plain, so far indeed that its outlines were vague and unsure, their sharp eyes caught the movement of many men. First there was a long, sweeping line that fanned out on either side of a long thin column, and then, far back, behind all this, an irregular shape of isolated moving points of light.

'What is it?' said Math, looking at Gwydion in fear.

The other boy's face was deadly serious. 'I know what that is. I have had to draw diagrams of them in school. That is the Roman army – the cohorts in that column, the horse-riders, the Alae, on either side of them, and the baggage and siege engines coming up behind. That's a Roman army, all right, I can tell you, and they mean business. There must be many thousands of men there.'

Math said, 'Ought we to run back and tell your father?'

But Gwydion turned a look of amusement on him. 'Why do you think father has got ready? My people know all about this; their scouts have been bringing them word for days, no doubt.'

He began to tell Math about the Council meeting on the previous night, but pulled himself up short, for

that would lead on to the strange man-god by the woodside, and Gwydion had secretly promised not to tell a living soul about that.

Instead, he said, 'Come on, this way, we'll get a bit of hunting before the horns blow and we have to leave.' He tugged at Math's sleeve and dragged him over the crest of the next hill; and then, without warning, he stopped and flung himself to the heather, pulling Math down with him and clapping his hand over his friend's mouth to silence him. 'Sh!' he said. 'There are men over there, in the little hollow. Not Belgae!' Silently, the two boys crept slowly towards the lip of the hollow, Gwydion holding Bel tightly so that he should not give them away. They stopped behind a gorse bush which would shield them from the sight of those below, and then they looked down into the broad, ferny basin.

Three men sat playing dice, which they shook out of a bone cup on to a sheepskin, hide uppermost, spread

on the ground. The boys had never seen men like these
before. They were stoutly built and immensely broad,
and each had the same sort of face, square, determined,
hard-eyed, merciless. One of them was bare-headed and
the boys saw that his hair was shaven to the scalp, and,
like his companions, his face was smooth and sunburnt.

The two boys saw the round, polished iron helmets
with their hook-like chin-straps, the heavy leathern jer-
kins overlaid with plates of toughened metal, the short
leather kilt composed of straps that hung down over a
thick linen skirt; the stoutly soled marching boots; but
most of all they saw the long oblong shield, the thin,
vicious lance, the short, leaf-bladed stabbing sword.
There was no need to ask who these might be, they
carried their own name in their hard faces, faces which
feared no man, no animal, no country in all the known
world. These were men of the Legions, men who
marched half over Europe and Asia under the Eagles,
the greatest fighters that the world had ever known.

Gwydion shrank back. 'My father was laughing at
them last night,' he said. 'But these men are not like
those he was describing.'

Math said, 'Begging your pardon, Gwydion, you
Belgae are all the same. You laugh because you wish
to make a good impression, not because there is anything to laugh at!'

Gwydion gave him a stern look, but that did not
prevent Math from grinning, all the same.

'These must be scouts, come in advance to spy out
the land,' said Gwydion. 'They may have been about
here for days, for all we know. Why, we might even

have run into them when we were hunting yesterday.
It is a frightening thought. I wonder what they would
do, if they caught a boy?'

Math smiled wryly. 'I have never heard that the
Romans were famous for their gentleness,' he said.
'They are soldiers, and have no thought in their shaven
heads but for fighting and looting. If they caught you,
my dear friend, they would just strip the gold ornaments from your neck and arms and then . . .' And Math
made the same gesture which the guard at Camulodunum had made the night before. Somehow, it seemed
more horrible when Math made it, and Gwydion turned
away.

Just then, Bel gave a whimper and broke from his
master's hands. The dog had almost run into the hollow when he saw the strangers and turned back to the
boys.

'Come on!' said Math, already on his feet. 'They
have seen Bel and they will know someone is near. Look,
they are coming up the slope!' There was no time to
lose; the boys ran as fast as they could, and had just
fallen into a fern-hung ditch as the first Roman javelin
appeared over the top of the hollow. Covered with fern
fronds, they lay still, Bel clasped securely this time, with
Gwydion's hand round his muzzle, shivering with
excitement.

At last, on either side of them, they heard the sound
of heavy footsteps, and heard men swearing in some
rough Roman dialect. Gwydion knew that they were
wondering who might have been with the dog, and
where it could have got to. Then he heard something

which sent his blood cold. The leader of the scouting party had said, 'What if they are in this ditch? Give it a prod, you men. We'll soon see!' Then the boys heard the sound of those cruel javelin points thrusting through the fern fronds, coming down the ditch on either side, towards them. Gwydion actually felt the dry leaves shake a little to his side as the bright knife-edge cut through them. Then suddenly the thrusts stopped, when they were but a foot from the boys; and away from the distant hill came the long blasts on the war-horns that Caswallawn had told his son to listen for. The Romans paused and listened, then they spoke to each other hurriedly, and began to move away a little, debating what they should do. One man was for making a more thorough search of the hill; the others were all for probing the length of the ditch again, on the chance that they had missed their quarry in their first search.

The boys lay still, almost choking in their efforts to be quiet under their layer of grass and fern fronds. The horn sounded again; that would be the final warning, Gwydion knew. The wagon would be leaving now, without them. Yet the Romans were still talking above them, and the boys knew well enough that these were men without mercy; not the sort to take pity on anyone, much less the children of the enemy they had come so far to destroy.

It seemed like an eternity before the Romans concluded their argument and went a little distance away, to sit down and wait, for from what Gwydion could make out, they intended to hold their position on the hill until the cohorts had moved very much nearer, and then they would go down the hillside to meet them.

Gwydion reached through the bracken and clasped Math's hand, as though reassuring the slave that they must stay there and think of a plan afterwards.

Then Bel began to struggle again and Gwydion's energies were well occupied in keeping the dog still. He almost took out his heavy sling-shot, in desperation, to stun the dog, for he felt that even this might be better than all of them meeting a certain death. But luckily Bel became still again and Gwydion's hand moved away from his belt.

Gradually the sun climbed overhead and began to burn down into the ditch. The boys became almost unbearably thirsty. Then the soldiers began to whistle softly, and even to sing in low voices – songs which were not in Latin at all, but in a number of languages and dialects. In fact, the languages of the various countries in which these tough soldiers had marched during their many hard years under the Eagles. And some of the choruses sounded so inviting that once Math almost forgot himself and began to join in. Gwydion heard the sound start in his throat and wondered whether this would be the signal for the Romans to throw a spear or two into the ditch to make sure that no one was hiding there. Yet even through his fear he sensed the power, the arrogance of Rome, that her soldiers should dare sing her songs while out surveying in unexplored enemy territory. These Romans were brave men, whatever else one said against them, thought Gwydion.

Then at last, perhaps an hour later, or even more, a

new sound came floating up the hill to the tense ears of the hidden boys; a low whispering rhythmic sound, a shuffling sound that at last resolved itself into a definite beat, a marching beat. It was the sound that had struck fear into half the world, the sound of an approaching Roman army. Mingled with this frightening sound of feet came the many other sounds of a moving army; the neighing of horses, the shouts of officers, the clash of arms and armour and the thin high screaming of the terrible Roman trumpets.

Even Gwydion felt his pulses race as he heard this strange intoxicating sound. This was what his father would hear soon; this was the last sound that many brave men, on both sides, would hear before that fateful day was out.

Then suddenly the Romans on the slope above them began to shout and cheer, and call out their regimental war-cries. Then the boys heard the thudding of their footsteps and their spears rattling against their shields as they ran, and they knew that their pursuers were gone.

The lads waited for a while, and then slowly raised their heads above the ditch. No one was in sight, and a rise in the hillside blotted out their view of the plain below. They could not see the Roman army.

At last Gwydion whispered, 'It would not take us long to catch the wagon up, for they will go slowly, expecting us to follow. It seems a great shame to be so near a real battle, and not to see what it looks like. Shall we go down and see what is happening? Are you willing, Math?'

The dark slave nodded his head. 'But do not hold me responsible, Gwydion,' he said. 'It is your idea, not mine.'

'Very well,' said the Belgic boy, 'I will take the blame. Come on, we must keep our heads down, I don't know quite where the soldiers are. They sounded close, but with as many men as that, the sound of their feet would be bound to sound near, even though they were a mile away.'

And so the two boys made their way down the hill in order to witness the battle of Camulodunum, and the invasion of Britain by the great general, Aulus Plautius, with almost sixty thousand men; though they were not aware of this; nor would it have meant a great deal to them had they been aware.

5 · Ha! Among the Trumpets!

Under the summer sun that day the fate of a country was to be decided, and the two boys, watching from a hillock over half a mile away from the conflict, gazed with set faces, their hearts beating with excitement. Even Bel was caught up in this frenzied atmosphere and, as trumpets blew from the Roman side and the long war-horns howled from the Celtic side, the small hound leapt on his thong-lead with an excitement as pronounced as that of his young master, whining and scratching the springy turf, as he tried to break away and run from this immense turmoil which now seemed to approach and now retreat from the watchers on the hill. Down there it seemed that half the world had assembled to do battle, for the plain was now dark with a multitude of men.

The Roman cohorts were in position now, the sturdy, loud-voiced centurions and decurions pushing and beating the headstrong legionaries into the formation they required; the noble young officers, with their red horsehair plumes floating in the breeze and their blue cloaks puffing out behind them like smoke, galloping from company to company, calling out now and again, and pointing here and there with their gilded staffs or long cavalry swords.

The infantry of the Legion was in place, solid and waiting, each man bearing his shield well before his body, his long lance held up and slightly pointed forward, ready for the command to advance.

Then a great hush settled over the tumultuous preparations, for there was a series of blasts on the long silver trumpets, and line after line of Roman archers marched forward, past the waiting ranks of infantrymen, accompanied by cheers as they went, each man with his head held proudly and erect, to take up their positions at the very front of the foremost line, protected only by one rank of shieldmen.

Gwydion watched them in admiration, as did the various groups of Celtic tribesmen who sat, here and there, facing the Romans, on the broad plain. Gwydion looked over towards his own massed countrymen, and recognized many of the tribes by the colours of their tunics and plaids; Cantii, Trinobantes, his mother's own people, the Atrebates, even certain groups of Iceni, who had always spoken well of Rome in the past; but he noticed that there were no Brigantes, even though their old queen, Cartismandua, had been one of the first to promise help to Caratacus when his great father, Cunobelinus, had died a year or so before.

These tribes were all spearmen and swordmen and archers. The cavalry were out of sight, behind that high hill which lay over towards the city. So were the chariots, which would be led by the king himself. These would not go into action until the crowding, jostling footmen had had their opportunity of slaughter and plunder, for that was a standing agreement between the battle-leaders of various tribes.

Then, far from the rear of the Roman multitudes, came riding men in coloured skin tunics, and high sheepskin hats, each one with a feather, and usually a heron's feather, stuck in its point. Gwydion stared at them, at their long horn bows and little shaggy ponies, and he gasped. For now he knew what that man was whom he had seen in the wood that night – a Roman horseman, a wild rider from Scythia, and not a god at all! And as his mind went back, he wondered whether the man he had seen was a spy, or a deserter from Rome, a horseman who was tired of serving a heartless Empire that, at the end of his twenty years of service would offer him little more reward than mere citizenship of Rome. ... But Gwydion's thoughts were rudely shattered then, for, with a wild skirling of horns and beating of gongs, the Celts opened the attack, moving swiftly down the hill in small vicious groups, like a great cloud shadow on a sunlit day, harrying the enemy at various points and in various ways, some with the spear, some with bows, and some with knives, at close quarters. Yet though the tribes always left heaps of dead, their own and those of Rome, behind them, the formation of the Legions did not falter, and the shield-wall stayed, as solid as before.

Here and there among the widespread tumult the boys saw the tribesmen tearing off their clothes and armour and, singing a wild death song, begin to dash across the stony plain towards the stolid ranks of Rome. Sometimes, as these madmen approached, their enemies cheered them on, and even laughed at them, until they fell, pierced by sword or javelin, a yard or two from the impregnable shield-wall.

This sporadic fighting might have gone on for long enough, with the archers and the shaggy horsemen waiting, smiling superciliously, and the great gold Eagle of the Legion still shining proudly in the afternoon sun; but then something else happened. Suddenly there was a shower of rain, which beat down out of the summer sky without warning, and in the midst of it appeared a great, brightly coloured rainbow that seemed to arch itself immediately over the Celtic tribes. A great whisper of wonder rose from the armies, a sound like the hissing waves of the sea on a rocky shore; and the massed tribesmen seemed to shudder as they drew back and fell to their knees, many of them, offering thanks to their gods for this omen of victory. Then the shower passed as suddenly as it had begun and the rainbow went with it, leaving the battlefield a place of great stillness and expectation.

Then, before the footmen of the tribes could regain their feet to attack again, there came the high wailing sound of the king's own war-horns, the signal for the chariots, and to the wonder of the boys, there rose above the hill the many-coloured pennants of these carts of death.

'Look, oh look!' said Gwydion aloud. 'The king has come! The king has come, and my father will be close to him in the battle line!'

Then, as the boy had said, foremost in the long line came the ebony and gold chariot of Caratacus, its red dragon flag furling and unfurling as the winds caught it and let it go again. At the king's right hand, and smiling at his master, stood Gwydion's father, Caswallawn, holding the reins lightly and waiting for the signal to charge. Gwydion stared at the family chariot, for it looked so different now, so dangerous and even wicked, though he had played on it, climbing in and out of it in the stables for as long as he could remember, and he had never thought of it as being a cruel weapon of destruction before. Now it thrilled him that his house should be so represented, and so near to the king too. He saw the golden-haired Caratacus, with his great horned golden helmet, turn and say something to his father, and the chariots manoeuvred close together so that the two men could shake each other by the hand.

'Did you see that!' said Gwydion in an ecstasy. 'Oh, I wish I could be with them today! Don't you, Math?'

But Math stared, dark-eyed and serious, for he was watching another people, not his own, and he did not see the fine glory of it all, as Gwydion did. He did not answer.

Then the king took the red dragon banner and took it in his hands, and whirled it round his head, once, twice, and on the third sweep flung it high into the air. A gasp of wonder broke from the Roman ranks. Then down came the banner and Caratacus caught it and shouted. And from the throats of all the tribesmen came the great deep shout, 'Caradoc! Caradoc! We are your dogs, who wish to die for you! Caradoc! Caradoc!' Math had time merely to glance at his friend, and to note the tears of glory that stood in his light-blue eyes, and then the chariots began to roll forward, slowly at first, for the charioteers found it difficult to manage their restive horses who knew that they were in battle again after many months of idleness in field and barn.

Then, like some monster slowly gathering speed, the chariot line moved, first at a walk, then at a canter, and at last at a gallop; and from the massed cohorts

came sharp orders and the sudden screams of the Roman trumpets. In his excitement, Gwydion moved from the shelter of the rock behind which he had been standing, and ran out into the open. Math followed him, himself almost caught up in the magic of the battle. Then came the clash, and for a while there was nothing but a vast maelstrom of shields and spears and charioteers tumbled in the dust.

Gwydion scanned the broken line and saw that his father and the king were safe. Then he looked at the Roman line, but all the spaces had been filled, and it was as though there had been no charge. The chariots retired for a while, drawing back a hundred paces, while the footmen went in again, hacking and stabbing and trying to break the first shield-wall. Then they, too, withdrew, leaving many of their comrades behind them, and once again the king waved his red banner; but this time, before the charge could roll forward on its way, a strange thing happened – the shield-wall seemed to melt away, the line of men swinging like a great gate, to right and to left, leaving exposed the archers, each one erect and bearing his bow drawn to

its full and directed towards the Celts. There was a
sudden call on the horn and a shout from a centurion
who controlled the archers, and the air was full of the
hum of arrows, as though a great beehive had suddenly
been kicked over and the angry swarm had rushed out
to avenge the outrage. Charioteers toppled from their
platforms, axemen who stood on the central shaft between the horses fell, clutching their throats or their
chests; horses snorted and sank to their knees. Then
the shield-wall closed again and the archers were hidden.

'A Roman trick,' shouted Gwydion. 'The trick of a
wicked people!' But Math did not know what to
think; he clasped his friend's hand tightly, and looked
to see that Caswallawn was still safe, still beside his
king.

So the chariots moved again, those that were left, and
once again the shield-wall took them, swaying a little,
breaking here and there, but never collapsing. This
time, before the chariots might withdraw again, the
final stage of the drama was enacted. The Roman commander had sized up the Celtic method of attack, and
now acted as he thought fit. There was a long thin
scream on the trumpet, and from either side of the
cohorts came the galloping of hooves and the high wild
shouting of the little Scythians, their sheepskin hats
bobbing in the wind, their bows ready bent, their
barbed arrows already flying into the whirling mass of
the disorganized chariots. Gwydion saw his father go
down, and watched the Romans run forward to him,
thrusting with their javelins again and again, as the

Scythians swept round and round, shooting as the desire took them now, at all fugitives. Math saw the king's chariot swing round, the red banner trailing tattered behind it, and gallop fast towards the brow of the hill. A few Scythian horsemen tried to follow it, but they were dragged from their ponies by equally savage tribesmen who formed a rearguard after their defeated master. Then Math heard Gwydion give a great sob and a shout, and saw that he was running down towards the thick of the battle. He did the only thing a friend could do, and followed him, Bel now running free at his side, his thong-lead dragging behind him.

6 · The Beasts of Doom!

Gwydion found himself running, almost as though in a dream, hardly realizing that his feet were touching the hard ground. The chaos of battle seemed to involve him, many strange sounds buffeted his ears, the shouts of men, the neighing of horses, the screaming of many trumpets. Then he saw the great siege engines looming over him as he ran into the thick of the surging masses – the giant catapults and slings, the grim and ornamented battering-rams that would never need to be used now. He skirted their threatening shapes and found himself among men, men groaning and swearing and praying to their many gods, and was carried hither and thither like a frail cork in a turbulent stream. He saw swords and lances moving about him, and banners floating over his head, but he did not once stop to think that he might be putting himself in danger; all that was in his mind now was to go to his father, whom he had seen tumble from the chariot, already limp, his head thrown back, his helmet falling off.

Once the surging sway of the conflict carried him towards the great heap of war-carts that had crashed into each other when those fearful arrows had taken their toll. He even recognized their own chariot as he moved past it as in a nightmare; he thought he saw his father lying across a broken wheel, his broad chest pierced in many places with red-hackled shafts. Then his eyes misted over, and had he not been swept along by the mixed crowd of Cantii and Romans, stabbing and cutting at each other desperately, he must surely have fallen in a faint on the ground. Then, amidst all this clamour and confusion, his benumbed senses were aware of a new sound, a strange urgent trumpeting, a cross between a roar of anger and a shrill cry of agony. It was a sound that he had never heard, or hoped to hear, before. Then the men about him seemed to scatter, to fade like a morning mist before the first gusts of day. A great space was cleared about him, for the men had fled, and now he saw this new horror which had cut through them like a deadly scythe. A long line of fantastic beasts was thundering down upon the remnants of the Celtic forces; great hunched beasts, with trunks and tusks, and armoured headgear, from the centre of which long murderous spikes projected, to pierce all who could not make their escape, Celt or Roman, it did not matter which. And on the shoulders of each of these beasts sat a negro, dressed in coloured finery, grinning and shouting hoarsely, encouraging the elephants which had never before been used in battle on the soil of Britain.

Gwydion stopped in his headlong rush, staggered as the beasts rumbled towards him, tried to run before them for a pace or two, and then, from fear and exhaustion, slipped and fell to the trampled earth.

So he lay, half-unconscious in terror, while the ground about him shuddered with the impact of those immense feet. He did not dare to wonder whether he would live or die; he only lay still, and sobbed on the dusty soil, all the fight gone out of him; and at last something struck him on the head and in the middle of the back, and he knew no more.

7 · The Good Centurion

It was night-time when the boy regained consciousness. He sat up and looked about him, shaking his head, for he was still dazed. He was in a three-sided tent, it seemed, the fourth side being open to the night. Fires were burning here and there outside, and men were passing to and fro constantly, Romans, and their henchmen auxiliaries, many of them dressed in sheepskins, as though they had come from a cold climate to fight with these Roman invaders.

Although his head and back were still rather painful, Gwydion turned and peered through the torchlight to

see who was in the tent with him, for he was aware of
whispering sounds, and of occasional moanings from the
darkness behind him.

Lying against the far wall of the tent were perhaps
half a dozen men, some quite young, still clad in their
Celtic finery, though now sadly bedraggled and war-
worn. A few of them were wounded and nursed their
arms or legs, in pain. Then one of them, a dark-haired
boy, got up and came over to Gwydion, smiling sadly.
It was Math.

'Oh, I am glad that you are alive,' said the slave. 'You
have been lying still for so long, I feared you had been
killed when the javelin struck you.'

Gwydion said, 'Was it a javelin then? I thought it
was the foot of one of those great beasts.'

Math said, 'If the Emperor's elephants had trodden
on you, I should not have bothered to sit here waiting
for you to come round! No, it was a badly thrown
javelin, loosed by one of the retreating Cantii. It did
not strike you properly, at its full strength, but flat,
when it was almost spent. You have a thick skull, Gwydion, luckily.'

Gwydion tried to get up, but fell back again. Then
he knew that he was bound, by waist and ankle, with
thick, horse-hide thongs, to the centre tent-pole. He
noticed that Math was bound by a long strip of hide
to another pole; and so were all the others in that tent.

'What are they going to do with us?' he asked.

Math said, 'We are prisoners, Roman slaves.'

Gwydion tried to leap up once more. 'I am no slave,'
he shouted. 'I am a free-born man of the Belgae!'

At the back of the tent, some of the others laughed, for they had been conscious while Gwydion had slept, and they had had time to become accustomed to their new state of servility.

Then Gwydion began to weep bitterly for the death of his dear father and the loss of his freedom. Math came to him and put his hand on his shoulder. 'Never fear, friend,' he said. 'Slavery isn't so bad, if you can only find a good master.'

Gwydion said, 'It is different for you. You have never known what it was to be free.'

Then he saw that he had hurt his friend, and took Math's hand and tried to indicate that he was sorry, though he was too full to say so with his voice just then. But even as he held his friend's cold hand, a shambling figure passed the tent, a Scythian, dragging a dog on a long leather thong. The dog was protesting and hanging back, and the man was shouting at him, and pulling cruelly on the lead. Gwydion's heart leapt. 'There's Bel,' he cried. 'They've captured Bel! Bel! Bel!'

Once the dog tried to turn towards his master's voice; but the wild Scythian forced him to follow, and then they were out of sight, at the other side of the tent. Now both boys gave way to their feelings, and made no attempt to hold back the shameless tears which coursed down their cheeks. This was the final degradation, felt Gwydion, that his dog, his own hunting-friend, should be taken from him by a wild man of the Steppes, a man who was little better than an animal himself.

Outside, the many noises of the camp were stilled a

little as night came on fully; though from one direction or another came the sound of victorious soldiers, singing and dancing and blowing upon their strange Roman horns. It all sounded very uncouth and different to the boys, and now they began to feel very homesick and lonely, even though they were in their own land, and indeed only a few miles from their own home.

At last a negro slave-woman brought in bowls of something like porridge, flavoured with cinnamon. The boys took it and ate, for they were desperately hungry by now. Gwydion made a wry face at his, but Math shrugged philosophically, for he knew that a slave must be thankful for what he can get; a prisoner must not desire to pick and choose what he shall eat and drink. He must take what is given, and thank the gods.

Some time afterwards, a big soldier entered the tent and stood looking down at them all. Gwydion could see from his helmet-tuft that he was a centurion, quite an important man, though not an officer like those who had ridden round the cohort with their red plumes trailing, that afternoon.

This man was broad and powerful, though kind-faced. His hair was grey and grizzled at the sides of his helmet, under the chin-strap, and the lines down his tanned face made him seem older than he was. His nose was beaked and stern, but his deep-set grey eyes twinkled as he looked down at the prisoners.

'Did they give you enough supper?' he asked, in a rough Celtic dialect, a dialect of southern Gaul, Gwyd-

ion decided. Not one of the proud Belgae would answer him. The prisoners stared at the ground and would not even look up at him.

The centurion sighed and shrugged his great shoulders a little.

'I can understand your feelings, my friends,' he said. 'It is never good to be defeated, and you folk have had little practice in the art of accepting defeat, I know. I should know, I've been fighting Celts in one place or another all my life, it seems! But come on, cheer up, life is never as bad as it seems. You could have done worse than be beaten by Rome! After all, we are worthy opponents, even you must agree!'

He waited for them to laugh, or perhaps chuckle; but there was a dead silence in the tent.

He tried again. 'You are prisoners, and you will be sold as slaves, somewhere or other, in Gaul, or Rome, or even here. But take courage, a man need not be a slave all his life. He can buy his freedom, he can escape, or at the worst, he can put a decent end to himself if the chains grow too heavy to be borne. You Celts need to study the Stoics! Come on, cheer up.'

Gwydion looked up at him. 'I am Gwydion, son of Caswallawn,' he said. 'Today my father has been slain and my mother left a homeless widow. I have been taken prisoner when I should have been with her wagon, protecting her. These are excellent reasons why I should laugh, no doubt, sir?'

The soldier looked back at him and his face was grave. He was about to place his hand on the boy's shoulder, but sensed that Gwydion would regard this as an insulting familiarity. He drew his hand back again.

'My lad,' he said, gently, 'life can be very hard when one is young, especially if one is a Celt. Your life has taken a hard turn, I must agree; but you have many years left in you, and the gods may choose to cast their sun upon those years, if you will but be brave.'

Gwydion's eyes flared out at him. 'I am the son of a warrior, and hoped to be a warrior one day,' he said. 'Dare you, a Roman, speak to me of bravery. Why, if you would but untie my bonds I would show you whether I am brave or not.'

The Roman soldier smiled a little, but gravely, at this outburst, and so turned from the tent, for it was not good for him to be spoken to like this before the other prisoners. When he had gone, the others praised Gwydion, or began to moan over their wounds again. Math alone said, 'You should not speak to a Roman like that. You must remember that you are a slave now. He could have you branded on the forehead for saying that.'

Gwydion said in a rage, 'Math, you live for ever in the shadow of servility. My dog, poor Bel, has more spirit than you.'

This time he did not feel any remorse when he had spoken so harshly to his old friend. Nor did Math speak again, but shrank back into the shadow of the tent and stared before him hopelessly.

When an hour had passed, a legionary marched into the tent and shouted in too loud a voice, 'Is there a Gwydion here? Son of one Caswallawn, I think.'

Gwydion looked him in the eye and said, 'I am Gwydion.'

The soldier took out a knife and slashed through the boy's bonds and dragged him to his feet. 'Come with me,' he said, taking the boy roughly by the arm.

As they left the tent, Gwydion heard the others beginning to mutter, and he knew that they were wondering whether he would be branded for his insult to the centurion. But Gwydion was not afraid; he felt that he now stood alone in the world, and that, come what may, he had to show these Romans that a Celt was unbeatable, whatever the fortunes of war.

Then they stood outside a tent which was more splendid than the others, above which a pennant fluttered in the night air. A guard at the door presented his pike as they approached, then, seeing Gwydion, said, 'Push him inside. They are waiting for him.' He gave a laugh and lifted the flap of the tent so that the boy could enter.

Inside two braziers were smoking, thickening the air so that it was difficult to see for a moment; but at last Gwydion made out a young officer, his laurel wreath before him on a table, his head on his hands as he pored over a large roll-map that was spread out on a stand. He was a tired-eyed young man, with thin fair hair and a pale face. By his side stood the centurion, still in full armour, his sword resting in the crook of his arm, as though he was acting as personal bodyguard to this quiet officer.

Gwydion stopped before the table and stared the man in the eye, defiantly. He noticed that the Roman's

eyes were pale blue, like his own, and that his long thin
fingers were twitching nervously as he played with the
red tape that bound the map-roll, and which dangled
on to his desk.

The officer turned to the centurion. 'Yes, this is Gwydion,' he said. 'There's no mistaking the lad.' The centurion nodded and smiled.

Then the officer turned back to Gwydion and stared
him in the eye this time, and Gwydion felt his own gaze
waver before the piercing look of the Roman. He was
not as weak as he had appeared, Gwydion decided. But
the Roman smiled and said, 'Gwydion, my friend, I
have seen you before, a year or two ago. Then you were
a little boy coming to learn Latin in Camulodunum. I
was the military attaché at the court of King Cunobelinus, the father of Caratacus. I never expected to become a Roman officer in the field here, nor did I ever
expect to find that you were my prisoner.' He smiled at
the boy, but Gwydion stared past him to the back of
the tent. The officer made a small movement of the
hands, as though to say that he had expected the boy to
behave like this. Then he went on, 'My friend, I am
truly sorry for what has happened today. Your father
was a friend of mine, and has done me many good turns.
But war is apt to set one friend against another like this,
and in the heat of the moment, even the best of companions may try to do each other an injury. It is only in
the cool of evening that one's hot blood of midday
sees reason. I shall say no more, for you are a proud boy,
and I am a soldier of a proud empire. You are a prisoner,
a slave, whether we like it or not, you and I. That is the

fact; but I can make that fact more palatable to you, and I propose to do so. My good centurion, Gracchus, whom you know, has obtained my permission to buy you himself. It is irregular, for you should be presented for sale in the markets; that is the law of Rome. But Gracchus is my friend, and has often done me good service with his sword. He will buy you, and send you to Gaul, to Lugdunum, where he has a son about your age. There you could be his companion, and no doubt find many things with which to amuse yourself. What do you say, Gwydion?'

As Gwydion heard these well-meant words, many things came to his mind; his mother waiting, his father on the wheel, Bel, Math . . . Yes, Math! Now he was to become a slave to another boy, just as Math had been all these years. To be bullied and praised as his master thought fit. To be treated as a dog, when his master was out of sorts. . . . He looked the officer in the eye

'I would rather die,' he said, with all the pride he could find. Then, feeling the tears beginning to come to his eyes, he turned his head away so that they should not see them.

The centurion went to him and put his arm round his shoulders. 'Gwydion, lad,' he said. 'If you don't come with me, they will brand you and sell you in Londinium or Gaul. They might even sell you to some old galley-owner, as a rower in Antium. I want you to be a companion to my own lad. He is my only son, and you would be happy with him. He lost his own mother when he was a small lad; now he lives with my sister in Lugdunum. They are kindly folk. Will you come?'

Now Gwydion's pride would stand out no longer. He held the centurion's hand as though it were the hand of a friend, for the man did not seem like the terrible Romans he had heard of. This was a real man, like his own father, a kindly man at heart, a strong man.

At last Gwydion said, 'My friend Math. I cannot leave him. What will become of Math?'

The centurion glanced across at the officer, but the officer shook his head sadly. 'I cannot allow you two bargains, Gracchus! They could cashier me for that! I am sorry, old friend.'

'Will you come, Gwydion?' said the centurion 'I will send you by wagon all the way, and you shall not be chained if you will promise not to try to escape.'

Now too tired and too weak to protest, Gwydion nodded miserably. The centurion saluted the busy officer, who immediately went back to his map, and led Gwydion to the door.

'You shall sleep in my tent tonight,' he said.

Gwydion was very miserable now. 'Oh please, let me spend this last night with Math,' he said. 'He is my best friend. He will be unhappy that I have to leave him.'

But the centurion shook his head gravely. 'Gwydion,' he said, when they were well away from any soldiers, 'Math will not spend this night in the camp.'

Gwydion looked back at him in fear. 'What will they do to him?' he said.

The centurion smiled. 'Nothing,' he said. 'Not if he is as bright as I think he is. In an hour's time I shall push this knife under the tent to him. He will cut his bonds and escape. Perhaps he may even have time to cut the bonds of others of the prisoners who are fit to walk. Who knows!'

Gwydion saw the smile at the corners of the soldier's mouth, and he smiled too. 'Can I not escape with them, too?' he said.

The centurion replied, 'Not now we have that arrangement with the officer. No, do not frown, for I should not risk letting Math have the knife if you had not agreed to go to my son, in Lugdunum.'

And so it was agreed, and Gwydion accepted his part of the bargain. Before he went to bed in the centurion's tent, he asked if Bel could be found and returned to him, but although the centurion's men made a search, they could not find the dog anywhere in the camp.

In the morning, just after dawn, Gwydion was put into a wagon with four other trusted prisoners of rank, and was given a message by the centurion to carry to Gaius, his son, in Gaul. Gwydion was sorry to leave this friendly grizzled soldier; but he soon forgot that emotion when he heard a great outcry coming from the camp, for the escape of the prisoners had just been discovered.

The centurion looked up at the boy and made a wry face. 'Good luck go with you,' he said, 'and I hope there is a little left for me, for no doubt I shall be held responsible for that escape! You'd think I was to blame for everything that went wrong in the empire, to hear them talk, sometimes! Good-bye, Gwydion, and may we meet again one day!'

Gwydion waved until he could distinguish the noble grey head no longer, then he settled down in the wagon which was trundling south towards Londinium, from which port the prisoners were to embark for the crossing of the narrow sea.

Part Two

1 · The Fight by the River

As the heavy wagon rolled down through Gaul, Gwydion had much time on his hands, and often called to mind the events of his journey. He recalled Londinium, and the merry crowds that cheered the soldiers who marched alongside the big covered cart. It was hard to believe that they were Britons, too, for they seemed to welcome the invader. An old Belgic spearman who sat next to Gwydion in the wagon said, 'These Londoners are not true Celts. They are merchants, from all parts of the world. They welcome anyone who will bring trade, Roman or otherwise!' And he sneered at the citizens as they clustered about the tailboard of the wagon, until a foot-soldier threatened him and told him to be quiet.

Then Gwydion remembered that sickening crossing in a boat little bigger than a barge, although it had two tall hide sails, and four oarsmen at each side, captured sailors from Armorica. Gwydion was very sick, for the Channel was in a rough mood, and lay for two days in the scuppers without wanting to eat at all, though everyone tried to be kind when they heard who he was. There was an awful cross-current that delayed them, and the boat had to stray off-course in order to make any landing at all. They put in one wet morning at Gesoriacum, and even Gwydion brightened up a little to see

the tall lighthouse there that the Emperor Caligula had
built, years ago, when he had thought of coming to Britain himself. Gwydion had never seen a real lighthouse
before and was quite thrilled, until a boat-load of fishermen came out to tow them in and he heard their voices.
Then he was very sad, for they were Atrebates, of his
mother's folk, and they spoke just as she used to, slur-
ring their words lazily, as though the Celtic was too
much trouble for them to speak with care, not like this
precise Latin that Gwydion had been hearing spoken
so much since that dreadful battle.

But this mood of sadness soon passed, at least by day-
time, for the weather improved, and summer moved
into its richest phase as they boarded another wagon, a
smaller one this time, and began their journey south,
along river-banks and through narrow woodland paths,
stopping sometimes in little clearings and glades and
making fires, and living just like wandering folk from
Asia.

Gwydion's new guards were not very strict either, and
often let the boy roam about, hunting rabbits or wild-
fowl, as long as he reported back at the wagon before
sundown. Indeed, apart from his sorrow over his father
and Bel and Math, Gwydion often felt quite happy
again; until he lay down under his sheepskins in the
wagon, or outside under the axletree gazing at the
bright stars. Then his old sorrow came on him again,
and he felt very lonely among all these strange people,
in a foreign land. But these moods did not stay, fortun-
ately, and Gwydion grew quite excited when the
country became more hilly and deserted, and the driver

pointed with his whip towards the horizon. 'That's where we are bound for,' he said. 'We should reach Lugdunum by mid-morning tomorrow, unless we have some setback or other.'

Some of the older warriors in the wagon were chained and so could not enjoy the journey as Gwydion did. They only grunted and went on playing their games of dice, or telling old stories of battles they had fought in. But Gwydion felt a new thrill as he heard the driver speak the name – 'Lugdunum! Lugdunum!' Gwydion wondered what he would find there.

What he found at mid-morning the next day was a broad orderly town, its light stone buildings shining in the sun, its clean roads bordered by regular rows of trees. The citizens strolled about in the sunshine as though they were people of another world, a world which had never heard of Camulodunum, and Caratacus, and Caswallawn. Gwydion began to feel that he was a boy from some curious and primitive island, many hundreds of leagues away from civilization; yet always before he had thought that Camulodunum was the greatest city in the world. He somehow felt out of place in this bright, orderly town, and looked down at his grimy legs and dirt-stained arms, his ragged tunic and broken shoes.

Then he gave a bitter smile, and suddenly remembered that he was a slave; that he had not come to Lugdunum for a holiday at all, but to be the servant of a Roman boy, the son of the man who had helped to kill his dear father. Then, though the sun shone happily, and the doves cooed from the red tile roofs of the villas along the broad avenue, the Belgic boy was sad again, more deeply sad than he had ever been before.

And this sadness increased when, a few minutes later, they rumbled on to the low grey stone bridge across the broad river. A line of boys sat on the parapet, swinging their feet and whistling. As the wagon drew level with them, one of the boys, a sturdy lad with curly brown hair and a cheeky face, wearing a red tunic and a white hide belt, jumped off the wall and called to the driver,

'Hello, friend! What news from Britain? I am Gaius, son of the centurion Gracchus. Does my father send me a message this time, then?'

The driver nodded back towards Gwydion. 'He sends you a friend,' he said. The Roman boy strolled to the tailboard of the cart and looked up at Gwydion. 'A friend, eh?' he said. 'Is this a Belgic slave, this friend?'

The driver said, 'Aye, no doubt. He's a nice lad, and you'll no doubt become friends. You can take him if you make your mark on my list, to show that I have delivered him safely to you.'

Gaius made his mark as directed, and then said to Gwydion, 'Come on now, look lively. Have you got a message from my father? Where is it, man! Don't stand there like a moonstruck druid!'

Gwydion's anger flared up at these last words, for he had been brought up strictly at home to respect the druids. At first he thought of leaping on to the other boy and throwing him over the bridge into the deep river. A gnarled veteran, a charioteer, who had been kind to Gwydion during the journey, saw that look come into his face and laid his hard hand on the lad's wrist. 'Be wise,' he said. 'The time will come later.

There are many of us in Gaul, and one day we shall find the way to pay off old reckonings.'

Gwydion was comforted by these words. 'Good-bye, friend,' he said, proud to be treated as an equal by this old warrior. 'May we meet again, and may I be given the fortune to ride in your chariot.'

'Learn to use a bow, then, lad,' smiled the other. Then Gwydion jumped into the road and gave young Gaius the roll of paper, containing his father's message. The Roman boy grabbed it and turned away from his companions to read it, leaving Gwydion to stand alone and forgotten until he had come to the end of the roll. Then he turned and said, 'May the Gods be praised! We have gained a great victory over the British! Listen, my father tells how many chariots the Scythians over-threw with one volley . . .'

The boys gathered round him excitedly, gabbling and boasting of Rome. Gwydion turned from them and sat down heavily on a little stone seat by the parapet, the hot tears running down his dirty cheeks as he re-membered the scene which this short letter had recalled.

Suddenly one of the younger boys turned and saw him. 'Why, look,' he said, 'your slave's crying, Gaius! Your Briton is actually weeping!'

They gathered round him, jeering and pointing their fingers at him in scorn.

'Come on,' said another boy, a tall, thin youth. 'Let us give him something to cry about! Let us go down and dip him in the river!'

'Stop!' cried Gaius. 'My father says I am to treat him well! Leave him alone, I say!'

But the yelling group of boys took hold of Gwydion excitedly and dragged him from his seat, taking him unawares, and pulling him along the path and then down the bank at the side of the bridge. When he saw the broad river before him, he was overcome with fear, for his mother had followed the custom of her tribe and had once worshipped the river gods. He still remembered her telling him that one must not enter a river without first praying for the god's permission to do so; and now they were going to make him break that custom. He struggled hard, but they were too many for him, and soon he felt himself stumbling in the shallow water at the river's bank.

Then he did not have much time to think of the river gods, for the boys were ducking him down, and down again, standing up to their own waists in the river to do so. Gwydion's breath left him and he gasped, but they did not let go. Some of them were true Roman boys whose fathers were stationed with the Legion at Lugdunum; others were Gauls, who had been under Roman domination for so long that they regarded themselves as being different from their Celtic cousins of Britain. Gwydion could expect no mercy from them.

Once, as he came up for air, he heard the voice of Gaius, still shouting that they must release him immediately. But Gwydion took little notice of the Roman boy; he knew now that he must stand on his own feet if he was to survive. Then his right hand slipped from the grasp of his captor on that side, and with a desperate lunge, Gwydion reached out to the boy who stood nearest, catching him by the shoulder of his tunic. Exerting all his strength, he pulled the other on to his hip and threw him with all his remaining strength into the river. Then, as the boy struggled to rise, Gwydion pressed forward from those who held him and planted his foot firmly on the other's neck, holding him down.

At this, his enemies drew back a little, letting Gwydion's other arm go. At once he swung like a leopard, catching hold of the hair of his tall, dark tormentor, dragging him forward within reach. Then, with victory in his heart, he clasped the Roman boy about the waist and flung him to join his gasping companion into the stream.

Now the ring of boys drew away from him as he turned. The two who had tasted the delights of the river crawled out and lay on the bank for a moment, red-faced and spluttering.

Gaius, who stood away from them all, shouted, 'Gwydion, come here! Come to me!' But Gwydion's ears were full of other sounds now; the sounds of trumpets and the scream of elephants. And as the boys began to close in on him again, he yelled out, 'Up the Belgae! Up Caratacus!' and ran a few paces back so that he could have the pier of the bridge behind him. The boys came forward, savage-faced now, because of their lost pride. But Gwydion suddenly stooped and took up a piece of broken spar, as long as a sword, and as the first boy leaped at him, he brought it down with a thud on the shaven head. His enemy fell back, clapping his hands to the cut on his forehead. This enraged his comrades, who made a concerted attack now, and Gwydion had his work cut out to keep them off. Then, without warning, a stone flew from the hand of the tall dark-haired boy, striking Gwydion just below the eye and stinging sharply. He put his hand to the wound, and as he did so, three lads rushed him. Then a strange thing happened, for at his side, Gwydion suddenly heard the words, 'Up the Belgae! Up Caratacus!' He saw the boys reeling away from him, and turned to see that Gaius was alongside him, slashing out left and right, and shouting Belgic war-cries as though he were Gwydion's blood-brother and not his new master.

There is little more to tell of the fight by the bridge at Lugdunum. Their assailants moved away, rubbing their heads and their shoulders and vowing revenge on Gaius and Gwydion. Those two boys stood and stared at each other, a new friendship in their eyes.

'Why did you do that?' asked Gwydion. 'They are your friends.'

Gaius said, 'They are dogs; the sort of dogs who will only pull down their quarry when they are in great numbers. They are no true Romans. I had rather be a Celt than such a Roman!'

Gwydion was not sure how to take that last remark, but he smiled and shook hands solemnly with his new friend, and they began to make their way back to the road.

As they looked up, they saw that a platoon of Roman legionaries had halted to watch the fight, and were leaning over the balustrade to congratulate them as they reached the road. The decurion, a short, red-jowled man, clapped them on the shoulders as they staggered on to the pathway. 'Good work, lads,' he said. 'Get a

bit more meat on your bones, then come up to headquarters! There'll always be a place in my squad for
lads like you!' Gaius looked pleased; but the decurion
never knew why Gwydion gave him such an insulting
look. The decurion brooded over that look for the rest
of the afternoon, and then gave it up; you could never
be sure what lads were thinking, he said to himself!

So, arm in arm, the boys went to the home of Gaius,
so that Gwydion could show himself to the lady of the
house, the aunt of Gaius. She was a thin-faced woman
with grey hair and a sharp tongue, though kindly at
heart, thought Gwydion, as he noticed the little lines
that stretched down on either side of her mouth. She
dressed Roman fashion; with a long robe and a hood
that half-covered her face; but in all essentials, she was
neither Roman nor Gaul, but a citizen of the empire, a
member of that vast family of Europeans who owed
their solidarity to Rome. As soon as she saw the state of
Gwydion's clothes, and the colour of his arms and legs,
she bundled him indoors to bathe and put on a new
tunic, one of Gaius' thick linen tunics; for, as she said,
summer was getting to its close, and a lad must be wrapped up well if he was not to take a chill in this windy
valley. Then, when Gwydion emerged clean and well-
clad, she sat him down on a chair and looked at him
sternly, fingering his long fair hair.

'That will have to come off, my boy,' she said. 'We
can't have you the laughing-stock of Lugdunum.
Roman-fashion or nothing!'

Gwydion leaped up and looked round for a weapon,
but the look of anguish in Gaius' eyes was so great that

at last he gave in and let the busy little woman crop his hair short with her best scissors. She was not very good at this operation and often tugged his scalp as she snipped away at the thick hair; but Gwydion did not flinch. Yet, as he saw his bright locks falling to the mosaic floor of the kitchen, he felt almost sad enough to weep. Then he remembered that his father himself had once said what a nuisance in battle this long hair was, and how he wished the king would set a new style in warriors' hairdressing by having his cropped. Then, as he recalled these words, he did not feel so bad about losing his hair, and even forced himself to laugh at his new reflection, which Gaius showed him in a steel mirror that was kept on one of the tables in the kitchen for the use of the women slaves, who liked their own hair to be well-kept, in its plaits and braids, when they worked in the steam of the boilers and the heat of the great ovens.

So the boys sat down to eat together, and when twilight came Gaius' aunt got them both at her knee and made them promise to respect the house where they lived, and not to bring discredit on their family. She seemed to assume that Gwydion had accepted the family, in which he now found himself, as his own. The Belgic boy, overcome by all the unexpected kindness he had received, promised, as did Gaius, to do as the lady commanded. So they were sent to bed, in the same room, overlooking a little square courtyard where figs and grapevines grew under a sheltering wall that was ridged with terra-cotta tiles.

Gwydion found it hard to sleep that night, for the moon came in through the window-hole on to his face,

and the doves did not seem to wish to sleep, but kept up
their purring on and on into the night. At last he turned
over in bed, trying to settle down, and saw that Gaius
was also awake, watching him silently, with great brown
eyes. In the semi-darkness, he was very much like Math,
thought Gwydion; but now the positions are reversed –
I am the slave, and he is the master.

But Gaius put out his hand and took that of his slave.
'I am glad you have come, Gwydion,' he said. 'I think
that we shall get on well together, don't you?'

Those words made Gwydion feel even more sad, in a
strange way; but all the same, he fell asleep now, to
dream of the great fight under the bridge, but holding
the dark hand of his new friend almost till dawn.

2 · Death Knows No Friends!

This was a happy period for Gwydion in many ways.
Everybody spoke Celtic of some sort, and when they
found it difficult to make their meaning clear, Gwydion
could always manage a little Latin. He and Gaius would
spend many hours walking together along the riverside,
or sometimes even going away for a day at a stretch to
climb the misty blue mountains that encircled the shining town. They chattered away incessantly, for each
wanted to know much about the other's way of living;
from Gaius, Gwydion learned of Rome, and the story
of the great Legions, of the old gladiators and of the
Triumphs. From Gwydion, the Roman boy heard

strange tales of the stones near Sorbiodunum, and the sacrifices that went on each year on the dawn of midsummer day; of the scythe-wheeled chariots, the fierce warhounds of the tribes; of the Celtic gods of sun, and moon, and oak, and river. Gaius knew much of this already, for he was living in a Celtic land – but a land, nevertheless, which had lost many of its old customs, having been under the rule of Rome for so long.

All told, they passed the last weeks of summer happily, watching the squads of soldiers drilling in the square, and calling out cheeky comments to the decurions in charge; or swimming in the baths, near the river side; or occasionally helping, for the fun of it, in pulling grapes, or treading at the wine-presses.

Occasionally news came through from Britain. Gaius' father managed to send messages with the wagondrivers who passed that way, on their road to the Middle Sea. The boys learned that the Roman army had settled down near Camulodunum, and intended to make a permanent town there, slightly away from the old foundations; that the Belgic king had moved to the west, and that the Legion would probably have some tough fighting to do before the country was finally brought to its senses. Gaius was always very honest with Gwydion, and when there came difficult news like that, he would simply pass the paper on to his friend to read, without trying to hide anything; for Gaius was a true Roman, of the old school, who believed in telling the truth, in straight-dealing of every sort, and in honesty.

The best news that came through for them both was that Gwydion's mother had got away safely after the

battle and was living somewhere well to the west, beyond the great inland forests. The centurion had made
it his special business to find this out, for he knew that
Gwydion would be anxious to know about her. He
added the postscript that a certain Math was with her,
but that no dog had yet been found.

Gwydion was glad to know these things, and told
Gaius to thank his father in his reply. Then, one day,
a carter called at the house and asked to see Gwydion.
He handed the boy a small parcel, wrapped round with
bound sheepskin, and said that the centurion had commanded him on pain of death to deliver it to Gwydion personally.

Mystified, the boy unwrapped the package, and saw,
lying on the white fleece of the skin, his father's gold
arm-band, with the dragon-shapes embossed on its sides,
and enamelled in blues and reds and greens. The boy's
eyes filled with tears as he put it on his own arm. When
he tried to give the man a coin he had, the carter shook
his head and said that it was an honour for him to carry
out such a task. He then gave Gwydion a small roll of
paper, and took his leave. The boy unrolled the paper
and found that it was a note from the centurion, who
said gravely that Gwydion's father had been burnt on a
warrior's funeral pyre, as befitted such a man, and that
the Romans had provided a guard of honour at the ceremony. He ended by saying that Caswallawn's sword
had been sent, against all rules and regulations, to his
widow, if she would accept it, and if she could be found,
with the message that if ever she should be in need, the
Roman General, Aulus Plautius, pledged himself to

succour her in any way, and to arrange that she be granted citizenship and a house in Rome.

When Gaius and his aunt heard of this, they were very glad, and made a small feast to commemorate the good news. Half-way between joy and tears, Gwydion drank the rough red wine of the district, and ate the sweet honey cakes that had been specially cooked for him.

The next day, with the last warmth of summer still in the air, the plague struck Lugdunum, and the boys, returning home from a long ramble on the hillsides, found the aunt of Gaius leaning, pale and faint, against the fountain that played in the courtyard. When Gaius ran to help her, she waved him away, and told him to run for the doctor. Puzzled, the two lads ran, one in one direction, one in another, in case the first doctor might be out already with some patient.

When they returned a short time later, they found that the lady was lying on a straw-pallet, near to the fountain, with the slaves weeping around her still body. The doctor turned to Gaius and shrugged his shoulders. 'That is the way it is happening everywhere in Lugdunum,' he said. 'Such diseases come almost every summer. What can we do about it? She was a good woman. The gods will take care of her.' Then he shook hands with Gaius and went away.

The burial was very simple, for now there were so many dead in the city that hired mourners were impossible to obtain. A slave woman, who had loved the aunt dearly, risked infection to light the torches at head and foot of the straw-pallet, and to place a coin in the mouth of the dead lady, as was the custom. But there was no time for elaborate ceremony; there was no set funeral oration before the hall in the Forum, no sad blowing of horns, or procession of the family – who in any case, could hardly have been summoned from Rome at such a time, when diseases were rife within the city.

Instead, Gaius and Gwydion, together with the slaves, carried the body on its bier to the burning ground, outside the town gates, and there the ashes of the good lady were placed in a small marble urn, and set in the ground, among the many who had perished during the summer months.

As they made their way home again, a harsh wind blew up through the valley, chilling them both, and depressing their spirits. Outside the house they found a squad of soldiers and a junior officer. He almost ordered Gaius to let him in, and then, without removing his helmet, to indicate that he was speaking officially and not as a guest, he told the Roman boy that as the son of a centurion, with no relatives to look after him, Gaius must regard himself as the ward of the garrison in Lugdunum. His affairs would be administered by the officer commanding the garrison, and his slaves would automatically become the property of Rome, until such time as Gaius came of age, or his father was discharged from the army.

When he had delivered this message, he turned on his heel and walked to the door, stopping only to warn the boy that he must not sell anything without permission of the officer, and that he himself was to report weekly at the garrison to show that he was still in the

city and in control of his household. 'Otherwise, my
boy,' warned the soldier as kindly as he could speak,
'the State will be forced to appropriate your house and
belongings, slaves, goods and chattels of every sort.'
Then he smiled drily and went back to his men and
marched them off.

Gaius turned to Gwydion and said, 'Well, that looks
like the end of our friendship, doesn't it? You now belong to Rome, and not to me.'

Gwydion said, 'Can't your father do anything about
it?' For he had come to believe that the grizzled centurion was the master of any situation.

Gaius shook his head. 'The officer who spoke to me
just now is far superior to my father in rank,' he said.
'Besides, that is the law. We Romans live by the law;
and that is the law.'

Gwydion said, 'Now we are both slaves, of a sort,
friend. Both slaves of Rome, though you have a few
more rights than I have.'

Gaius said, 'Things look black, Gwydion, but we
must have courage.'

He even forced himself to smile at his friend, and
then they made up a big fire and brought their pallets
down to the kitchen, for it was becoming too cold to
sleep in the airy little room with the open window-hole,
above the courtyard.

3 · Through the Gates and Over the Hills

The next morning the two boys sat on the parapet of the bridge where they had first met, but this time clad warmly in sheepskin jackets and thick woollen trousers, strapped from ankle to thigh with broad thongs. The autumn days were becoming more chilly and it seemed that winter might be on the town sooner than they had thought. The morning sun struck down across the path, into the boys' faces, and they seemed at a loss to know what to say to each other.

Then suddenly Gwydion turned and waved his hand towards the misty blue hills that surrounded the city. 'There lies freedom,' he said, simply. Gaius looked back at him in astonishment. 'Why, that is just what I was going to say,' he said.

Gwydion said, 'Have you money with you?'

The Roman boy nodded. 'I have half a year's taxes that I was to deliver to the collector this morning after our walk,' he said, tapping the pouch at his side.

Gwydion said, 'We have on our winter clothes; we have strength in our legs and stout shoes on our feet. The hills mean freedom.'

At last Gaius said, 'If we stay here, we shall no doubt get into trouble of one sort or another. I imagine that since the house and stock belong to my father, a soldier, we shall be constantly plagued by the garrison now. Whereas, if we go, the officer will be forced to take over everything and keep it safe – they are very strict about such things – and we shall be relieved of much trouble.

You see, they would make us survey our land again and take inventories, put proper crops in at the right times according to the book, pay a terrific wage to any wandering journeyman who poked his nose round the door to scythe a field or cobble a cracked wheel. Then, they'd make us whip the slaves if they didn't work hard enough . . .'

He stopped as soon as he had spoken those words.

'I'm truly sorry, Gwydion,' he said, putting out his hand. 'My silly tongue ran away with me.'

Gwydion shrugged his shoulders and smiled back at him, a sad but friendly smile.

'Let us run away with it, my friend,' he said. 'That is the way to treat a wagging tongue!'

'Of course,' said Gaius, relieved. 'That is the only thing left for us to do, really. You know the way, Gwydion. Why, we might even get as far as Britain, to see my father.'

Gwydion said drily, 'I have a mother there, too. Britain is my own country. My people live there.'

Gaius flushed with embarrassment at his thoughtless selfishness. He was a little confused by Gwydion's Celtic touchiness, too. It was at moments like these that he realized the difference between the races. He did not know what to say now, but Gwydion spoke and said, 'I am now the slave of Rome, as even you cannot help reminding me, Gaius. What is the penalty for a slave who runs away from his owner? It is something which I must consider.'

The Roman boy's face became serious now. He thought deeply for a while and then said, 'Let us forget about running away, my friend. It was a foolish idea after all. The punishment is too great. Let us stay here, for I could not bear you to suffer like that.'

Suddenly Gwydion slipped down from the stone parapet. He stretched his long arms in the sun and yawned. 'Come on, Gaius,' he said. 'If we don't make an early start we shall not be over the hills for two days at the least!'

Gaius stared down at him for a moment or two, then slipped down after him. 'I had forgotten,' he said, smiling grimly, 'we both carry hunting-knives. Well, if they try to take us back against our will, we shall have something to say to them, whether they are Romans or not, shan't we, my friend?'

Passers-by turned in astonishment to see two young boys, arm in arm, striding whistling down the main street and laughing as though their solemn city were a place of vast delight and entertainment!

And so the two passed through the gates and up the road, turning off from the public carriage-way when they were a few miles from the town walls and cutting across the heather-covered slopes that led westwards, towards Armorica, the sea; towards Britain once again.

4 · Among the Veneti

As autumn turned to winter, and the trees now stood on hilltops like gaunt, black, foreboding sticks, the two boys travelled on slowly towards the coast. They soon discovered that even sheepskins do not keep out the cold when one has to sleep on the bleak hillside; that even stout shoes cannot withstand the hard flints of the road for ever; that even a half-year's taxes are soon spent, when one has to buy food, or a meal at an inn, or a ride in an ox-cart. For grown-ups in Gaul at that time were only too ready to cheat such boys as these, with innocent faces and a pocketful of coins.

Once they fell in with a strange old German who was walking from village to village with a dancing bear. They stayed with him for a few days, until they woke one night to find the old man searching among their clothing to steal their gold. Many times they had to hide hurriedly in ditches, or in the fringes of woods, when Roman cavalrymen came clattering down the road, or squads of infantry suddenly turned out of villages and marched in their direction.

Yet, at last, with the snow on the ground and a harsh wind whipping inland from the leaden grey sea, they came to a small hamlet perched high on a cliffside, and from the speech of the children who met them and talked to them, they knew that they were in Armorica, and, best of all, among the remnants of that rebellious old tribe, the sea-going Veneti. At first they were overjoyed, for it seemed now that they had but to go on board a sailing vessel, and the end of their long journey would be in sight. But they were doomed to disappointment.

Outside a tumble-down hovel of wattle and thatch, they saw an old man mending a fishing-net with shaking fingers. He wished them good day, in the courteous manner of these fisher-folk, but when Gaius asked whether he could take them to Britain, he merely laughed and then fell silent, as though they had asked him to fly to the moon and fetch them a bag of gold.

Gaius asked him again, thinking that he might be a little deaf; but still he did not answer. At last, rather impatient, Gwydion asked the same question. This time the old man looked up, recognizing a Celtic voice, and pointed out at the long grey rollers of the sea. Then he pointed down at the tiny fishing coble that lay, newly tarred, on the pebbled beach below them. He looked Gwydion in the eye with his pale blue sea-coloured orbs, and shook his head slowly. Then he went on with his work, and the boys walked away to another cottage, farther down the cliff.

There they had the good fortune to meet a stout, red-faced woman, whose arms showed that she was kneading flour for baking. She smiled at them and said they might came in and eat, for they looked hungry enough. They were glad to accept her invitation, and during the rough but generous meal, Gaius asked his question once more; was there any man in the village who would ferry them across to Britain, in return for gold that would be paid, one day, when the Roman army was shipped once more across to Armorica?

The stout lady said, 'Eat your bread, lad, and don't ask silly questions. Hereabouts, we don't care to be mixed up in the doings of Roman soldiers.'

Gaius didn't understand this, and felt a little insulted; but in a whisper, Gwydion, who knew a great deal about the history of his people, told him how the Veneti had been cruelly punished after their sea defeat in the days of the great Caesar, Julius. Moreover, he told Gaius that he had better let him do the talking from now on, while they were with such a folk as the Veneti, who were very proud, in spite of their poverty.

So Gwydion spoke to the woman, and showed her the arm-ring that his father had worn at Camulodunum. He told her his family history, and said that his mother was a great lady of the Atrebates, farther along the coast. The stout woman became interested instantly, and together they talked about various people of the Belgae and the Atrebates, and found that Gwydion's second cousin, Brochwel, was also distantly related to the stout woman's old chief, Bledyn, who had died only a few months ago when he was knocked from his horse by an overhanging bough on his way to a sacrifice at Carnac.

The stout woman made the boys have some meat which she had cooked, but had not shown them before; then she insisted that they drank a beaker of her best corn wine. She said that it would keep the cold out, and do them no harm. After that, she shut the door and said that if they had said who they were before, she would not have been so rude to them, and told them that her son-in law often made the voyage across to Vectis, although it was of course illegal, and he could be crucified for doing it if the Romans found out. She said that it would be little extra trouble for him to put the boys ashore somewhere quiet, to the west of Vectis, where the woods ran down almost to the waterside and they would be unobserved. Gwydion said that he would pledge himself to repay the man, and offered his father's arm-ring as security until the debt was paid; but the woman said she would give him a good slap where it really hurt if he mentioned money in that house again. So the boys stayed with her, until such time as the son-in-law should visit her, when she would arrange with him the voyage they wanted to make.

It was a very draughty little cottage indeed, its walls needing replastering so badly that the sea-wind seemed to blow straight through the wattle-sticks of which it was composed. But always there was a bright fire burning in the centre of the floor, made up with crackling dry seaweed and driftwood, and, wrapped in skins and thick lengths of woollen cloth which the woman wove herself in her leisure moments, they did not come to much harm from the cold, though it took them some days to get used to the thick smoke with which the hut was always full when the wind was blowing in a certain direction.

Often at night, when the darkness had settled on the little cliff village, the fishermen and their wives, and sometimes their children, would meet in one house or another, and there would be singing in the firelight, and the passing of the mead-cup, and even music from the pipe or the harp. The boys learned many new songs from these evenings; that is, songs which were new to them only, for in reality some of them were very old tribal songs, dating back to the time when the Veneti were a great maritime people, whose power had made the Romans exert all their severity in wiping them out.

The month of Januarius had come before the son-in-law put in an appearance, and the lads had come to think that they would never see this elusive young man. It was a bright frosty morning when he turned up, whistling up the side of the cliff, and bringing a bag full of fish for the stout woman, who seemed to think very highly of him, for they hugged each other so long that the boys began to feel embarrassed. Then it turned out that she had reason to be pleased, for the son-in-law brought her the good tidings that she was now a grand-mother, and that her new grandson was the very image of her, with a great mop of red hair already, and the brightest sea-blue eyes anyone had ever seen. The young man boasted proudly that this son would undoubtedly be a great warrior or a great fisherman, for he grasped at anything that was held near him, with a hand that was certainly made either for a sword or an oar.

Once again the fisher-folk were called in to cele-brate these glad tidings, and the mead cup went round the circle so often that no one thought of going out in the boats that day at all.

In the evening, however, when the house was empty of visitors once more, the stout woman told her son-in-law of the request that the boys, Gaius and Gwydion, had made. To their relief and surprise, he just laughed and said that they couldn't have come at a better time, for he was intending to sail in a couple of days' time, if the tides were right with the wind. He told them that he was taking swords and spears and other important weapons across to the Belgae, who would meet him near Vectis by the light of the moon. He said that since the Romans were pressing them hard, their sword-smiths were unable to replace all the weapons that were

needed, and that he performed this service in return
for certain things, like grain, and hides, and sometimes
even wine, which was difficult to get in that part of
Armorica. This son-in-law was a shameless trader, who
sold his wares wherever he could make a profit; he did
not try to hide this, though he assured the boys that,
as far as they were concerned, he did not want any recompense. Though, he added, it would be convenient
if both Gaius' father, and Gwydion's mother, could give
him a piece of paper, on which they said that he had
helped them at one time. This might be useful, he
thought, should he ever need support from either side.
The boys pledged themselves to have such papers made,
and sent to him, one day, and so he was contented.

It seemed to them that the stout woman was a little
cross with her son-in-law for this request, for she was
obviously more independent than he was; but the boys
well understood how, in those troublous times, these
fisher-folk had to grasp what opportunities presented
themselves, for it was every man's duty to look after
himself and his family, whatever the great military
powers were doing.

However, the next day the stout woman gave them
both a thick overjacket of rough tweed, and a package
of bread and dried fish, to see them through their voyage. She even added a flask of her most precious corn
wine, to warm them up at the night-time, as she said,
when the winds blew bitter-chill down that awful, cruel
channel.

So, in the late afternoon of the next day, they left
her and walked along the shore with the gay young son-

in-law, who told them that this was the quickest way to his boat, which was moored about five miles along the coast, in a tiny inlet which sheltered it from the prying eyes of Rome and her spies.

The stout woman stood on the cliffside, in the biting wind, waving to them until they were out of sight, her grey hair blowing across her kind, red face, and her ragged skirts whipped by the chill breeze that came straight from the grey and restless Atlantic.

5 · Death to All Romans!

When they saw it, the boys were rather disappointed in the boat which was to carry them over the dangerous winter seas. It rode but five feet or so out of the water, and did not seem the sort of craft to stand up against a vicious deep-sea roller. The son-in-law, who had pointed it out rather proudly, smiled when he saw the doubt in their eyes, and told them that this vessel had made worse voyages, in far worse weather, and that she would doubtless make others just as bad.

In general form, the boat was a blunt-nosed sloop, perhaps thirty feet long, and carried a square mainsail and a small triangular foresail, made of thin hides, pieced together with stout thread and well-greased for easier furling. Only the rear third of the boat was decked, and in this area the crew had their sleeping quarters. The undecked area of the boat was covered with a rough canvas awning which kept some of the water from whatever cargo she might be carrying. As extra motive power, there were four oars on each side; for use when the boat pulled inshore and sails could not be trusted.

The boys did their best to settle down away from the wind and the sleety rain below the small deck, crouching among the furs and skins and old woollen garments which the sailors had placed there in preparation for the night. Their guide, the son-in-law, went up on to the deck to talk with a foxy-looking, thin-faced man who seemed to have some authority in the venture and who was busy pulling the helm back and forth to make sure that it had not stiffened up or rusted in its sockets during the boat's period of idleness.

The other members of the crew, three sullen-looking longshoremen from another tribe, lounged about, cursing the weather and threatening never to make another trip unless their money was paid to them as soon as the arms were delivered on the other side.

In all, they did not seem to be a very trustworthy body of men. The boys had yet to learn the type of men who engaged in such illegal traffic. Nevertheless, the boat pulled out well enough, some time after the moon rose, and was soon well into deep water. They nibbled at the food which the old woman had given them, to pass the time a little, and wondered how long it would be before they set foot on British soil. They even began to talk of their people, Gwydion of his mother, Gaius of his father; it did not occur to them at that moment that this mother, and that father, belonged to opposite sides in the conflict.

Then, from above them, at the helm, they heard something which stopped their eating and conversation and brought them up with a jerk. The helmsman said, 'But they're a well set up pair of youths, Gryf. We could get good money for them. How do you know you'll ever get your piece of paper from the fair-haired one? And what's a piece of paper? We need money, good hard money . . . Roman, for preference, though I'm not particular!'

Only then did the boys realize what danger they had run themselves into, by coming out with men they had never seen before. Then the son-in-law spoke, and his voice had lost some of its carefree jollity, 'I've told you what I have to do,' he said. 'My wife's mother says they are to be set safely ashore. I must obey her, though I grant you these lads would fetch a good price. So forget it, and watch your steering; the patrols are liable to be out tonight, since there's a bit of moon.'

The boys stared towards each other in the dusk, wondering whether Gryf, the son-in-law, would have his way in the end; or whether the crew and helmsman would force him to adopt their plan of taking the boys to some market, to sell them as slaves. Then, suddenly, there was no more time to speculate on their future fate, for a shout from the crew sent the boys running to the side of the boat.

A mile to the port side they saw a pitch-ball shoot up, a fire flare, to be answered on their other side by another, this time very much nearer.

'What are they?' asked Gaius.

'Roman patrol boats, son,' said a sullen seaman, spitting into the water, which was even now coming high up the side of the craft. 'We may have to run for it,' the man went on. 'Either that or give ourselves up, and hope to escape when they clap us in gaol. We've done that before now! Haven't we, mate?' He addressed a one-eyed villain who lounged beside him, his face grim, but unconcerned.

'We'd better not do it again,' this man replied. 'We'll lose our ears if they ever catch us again!'

Gaius looked hard at his friend, thinking that if they were caught, poor Gwydion must take the harder punishment, for he was a runaway slave in the eyes of the law.

Luckily they found a strong cross-wind which bore them offshore rapidly, and out into open sea. Gwydion saw that they passed close to some small islands on the starboard side, where flares seemed to be lit on hillocks, possibly to serve as beacons for incoming Roman sea traffic, for the invaders liked to have their sea-routes as well-managed as their roads, when they could, and when the barbarians did not douse the flares purposely, so as to make their Roman masters run aground.

After a while, Gryf came and told them to take shelter again. Gaius said, 'Is there going to be a fight?' But the man laughed, 'No, we shall be striking rough water soon,' he said, as he went back to talk with the helmsman once more.

'We dodged them,' said the one-eyed sailor. 'They won't come out as far as this; though no doubt they'll be waiting for us when we come back! But we can deal with that when it happens.' He began to laugh and nudge his companion, who punched him back, rather hard; after which the two rolled about among the cargo, pretending to be angry with each other. The boys could see that these were very hard men, who cared for no enemy, and who fought among themselves if there were no Romans to fight.

Neither of the lads slept much that night, for the waves rolled the clumsy craft about cruelly, until at last the sails were taken in so that the ship might not heel over completely. Even the sour-faced helmsman said that it was a bad night. But shortly after dawn

broke, the boys fell into a deep sleep, partly from
hunger and exhaustion, partly from the rocking motion
of the craft, which had now settled down to a steady
rhythm since it was making little way, and seemed
merely to be bobbing up and down on the waters.

When they woke, it was quite light, but the sea was
shrouded by a heavy fog. The son-in-law brought them
a bowl of broth, which had been warmed on a brazier
lighted on the deck. He told them that it was great good
fortune that this mist was so thick, for now they stood
less chance of being seen by Roman galleys. The boys
noticed that the sails were again set, and that they
seemed to be making fair progress, though there was
but little wind. The crew lay snoring in various parts of
the boat. Gryf said, 'They're tired. They had to do a
bit of rowing when you two had gone to sleep. Perhaps
you'll have to do some, too, before we reach Britain!'
He laughed and then left them to eat their scant meal.

Nothing eventful occurred that day. The boys exam-
ined the cargo, and saw that it consisted chiefly of rough
swords and spear-heads. They handled some of them
and decided that they were far inferior to anything
that they had seen before. 'Beggars cannot be choosers,'
said Gwydion. 'A warrior needs a weapon immediately;
he cannot stop fighting to make one!' Nevertheless, he
knew in his own mind that these things would cut a
poor figure against the highly tempered and accurate
weapons of Rome.

Towards the bows of the vessel, there were a group
of barrels. These contained oil, to be used on the seas
as a means of weighing down the waves should they be-

come too troublesome. There were also many quite big
boulders, which acted as ballast, since this cargo was
but a light one. All told, there was little to attract their
attention on the ship, and they spent most of their time
lying in the warmth of the underdeck, and consoling
each other when sea-sickness threatened – which was
often during that day, and especially during the night,
when they ran once more into a rough sea.

On the third day the weather cleared and the seas
were kinder. The helmsman handed over his duty to
Gryf, the son-in-law, and came to sit with the boys as
they ate what they could, shuddering now with the
chilly morning breezes.

'We shall not be long now,' he said. 'It has been a
quick crossing for the time of year. Gryf and me have
been out here when it's taken us four or even five days
to make this trip. You lads are lucky. You must be born
for great things!'

He laughed, yet still Gwydion did not trust him, and
felt that should anything happen to Gryf, the helmsman
would not have any scruples about selling them into
slavery to any bidder, Celt or Roman. Still, he smiled
back at the man, and decided to keep a sharp watch on
him, all the same.

As their luck turned out, that was not necessary. By
nightfall they skirted the long flat island of Vectis, and
ran out to sea a little to avoid any coastwise traffic. Then,
as they drew nearer the wooded coastline of the country
west of that island, they lay out for a while, at anchor
in the shallows, to watch for the arranged signal from
the shore.

It was during this wait that the accident almost happened. A light mist had got up and shrouded the surface of the sea for a height of three or four yards. Almost at the moment when Gryf shouted, 'There it is! I can see their flares in the woods!' Gaius glanced over the side of the sloop to see a sharp-nosed launch pulling towards them silently, half-hidden by the mist. In what moonlight there was, he discerned the gleam of helmets and spears. There was no mistaking the identity of that trim craft; it was a Roman coastal patrol, and it had sighted them well and truly. They could not have pulled up the anchor, much less have got under way before it closed with them.

The boys were excited then to the point of fear; but the sailors seemed to take it all very calmly. For a moment, Gwydion, who was more accustomed to the treachery of the tribesmen, thought that these sailors might well decide to barter their passengers for their own safety, but he did not confess this fear to Gaius. Instead, he stood with Gryf and the helmsman on the half-deck. They were silent and smiling. The crew were sitting on their haunches below the awning, as though nothing was happening of note.

'What will you do?' whispered Gwydion, his teeth chattering. The son-in-law grinned and said, 'It could be oil; it could be ballast!' Then he began to smile again, and Gwydion did not dare ask for further information.

Then the Roman boat grated alongside and the officer stood up, his thick cloak pulled up to his chin, but his sword ready in his hand. Gwydion thought that he looked a very harsh man, who would show little mercy towards any enemy of Rome.

His voice was just as hard as the boy had imagined it might be. 'Stand still, all of you!' he called. 'Where are you from and what have you aboard?'

Gwydion saw that there were three archers in the launch, with their bows already drawn, as well as two spearmen, who sat alongside the rowers.

The boats rocked on the tide, but Gryf stood quite firm, his arms folded and his mouth smiling pleasantly. 'We are men of the Veneti,' he said, 'and to tell you the truth we are carrying weapons to Britain, for better men than you are! Is that all you want to know?'

Gwydion heard the Roman officer make an exclamation of anger, then so much happened all at once that he did not see it all. He suddenly felt himself dragged to the deck, and saw that Gryf and the helmsman were beside him. At the same time he heard the arrows whistle harmlessly above their heads. Then, looking down, he saw two of the rough-looking crew pitch a massive boulder over the side of the boat. It landed in the launch even as the archers were fitting the next arrow to their string. The small vessel shuddered and heaved, the archers fell sideways; even the spearmen tumbled across the rowers, their javelins flying wide. The great ballast stone had plunged through the thin shell of the launch, and already the Romans were struggling with the treacherous currents, weighed down by their heavy armour, trying bravely to make their way to the boat and pull themselves up its sides. One man, an archer, got as far as the gunwale, but the one-eyed

Celt struck him heavily with a sword from among the cargo and he fell back into the water, without a cry.

That was what impressed Gwydion most of all, that these Romans did not seem to make a sound when they were fighting. They even suffered death in silence, it seemed. He admired that, and wondered what this crew would have done, had the positions been reversed.

Then he was conscious that Gryf was standing by him, smiling, his arms still folded. 'You would think that they knew that old trick by now,' he said. 'But these Romans never seem to learn the simple things. They are always on the look-out for some complicated move – and it never comes, at least, not from us! We either use ballast or oil!'

Gwydion looked so puzzled that the other said, 'If we have real difficulty with them we tip a barrel of oil on to them, and one of the men throws a torch into it. I have even pitched the brazier into it; but you can't always be sure of your aim when these launches carry archers. It's easier with javelin men; you can see them coming more easily!'

The boys looked at his smiling face, and shuddered. Gwydion remembered how pleased this man had been about his new-born son, and for a moment the boy wondered how a man could be so tender, and yet so cruel. He had yet to learn that when men go to war, they do not think of their opponents as being of the same nature as their own families.

Now the signal came again from the shore, and the anchor was lifted. The boat began to move slowly towards the distant beach. Gaius stood, still staring to-

wards the spot where the Roman launch had been, his
eyes vacant and wondering. Gwydion knew that he was
stupefied that his own great fellow-countrymen could
so easily be defeated by a group of untrained rogues like
these Veneti.

Then the boat grounded, and Gryf jumped into the
water and called to the boys to let themselves down into
his arms. He was enormously strong, and carried them
both to the shore, one on each arm. As he staggered
along with them, the waves lashing him waist-high, he
whispered, 'I had to take you both. I didn't dare leave
either of you aboard with him!' He nodded his head
back towards the helmsman, who stood watching them,
a disappointed expression covering his dark face. Gryf
went on, 'He'd be just as likely to set sail again and leave
me here, if I'd left one of you aboard. He'd make good
money from either of you!'

Then he laughed and said, 'You can't choose your
companions when you are a pirate like me! And he's
not such a bad fellow in the usual day's work!'

Then he tumbled the lads on to the sand, and wished
them good-bye. Gwydion called out that he would keep
his promise, and then they made their way towards the
wood that came down almost to the water. Under the
overhanging boughs, a group of men were waiting, and
Gwydion went expectantly towards them, for he believed them to be Belgae. But when their leader came
forward to look more closely at the boys, Gwydion realized his mistake. These were lawless men, wanderers, he
thought, who sold to the highest bidder and had no tribal loyalties. Their leader was a big man whose sandy

hair hung down in rat-tails from below an old skin cap.
His face wore blue woad-marks, and was tattooed hori-
zontally, in the fashion of the Picts. Gwydion observed
that he lacked two fingers on his right hand. This was
not a man whom he could trust, any more than he could
trust the others, that half-dozen of skin-draped savages
who stood behind him, whispering in the dusk.

The leader stopped before Gwydion and said thickly,
'Who are you? Have you come to join us?'

Gwydion spoke up boldly, taking a chance, and said,
'No, I am blood-brother to Gryf yonder, and am of the
Veneti. If you touch us, Gryf will come ashore and tear
out your eyes, never fear.'

Gaius put on as brave a face as he could, doing his
best to appear like a boy of the Veneti, though it must
have gone hard against his tough Roman grain to do so.

The leader sneered down at Gwydion and said, 'If I
chose, I should take you with me, Gryf or no Gryf!
What is to prevent me from taking you two now and
not stopping to unload the cargo in that boat?'

Nevertheless, the man withdrew back to his mutter-
ing fellows, and the boys then realized that this Gryf
was a man of some notoriety, in spite of his unprepossess-
ing appearance.

Yet it was obvious that they had little time to waste,
for they could not afford to travel with this band of
rogues through the woods that stretched before them.
Gwydion acted quickly; he tugged at his friend's jacket
and began to run inshore, away from these men. Luckily he struck a path, which made the going a little
easier, yet all the same the boys heard footsteps follow-

ing them for a while through the darkness, until at last, even these fell behind, and then the fugitives settled down to a rapid walk, unwilling to find themselves out of breath or exhausted when they might most need their speed. Nor did they stop, for more than a few minutes at a time, until dawn; but continued their journey northwards, as far as they could judge, until at last they came out into more open country.

Then Gwydion stopped as the first rays of the dawn sun struck through the leaden clouds to their right. 'Over there, far away,' he said, 'are the great stones. Now I do not know which direction we should take.'

This question was settled for them in a grim manner before they had travelled much farther, however. On the crest of a small hill, against the pale morning light, a well-harnessed horse was cropping the turf. There did not seem to be anyone with him, and Gwydion ran up the hill, hoping that he might bring the horse down without a fight for their own use. As he drew nearer, he saw to his horror that the gaily-painted Celtic saddle was covered with blood, and that the horse's flanks had been sadly gored by spear or short sword. He shrank back for a second, and as he did so, a weak voice from the coarse tussocky grass called out to him, 'Oh friend, do a soldier one last service.'

Gwydion beckoned to Gaius, who ran after him towards the voice. A Belgic cavalryman was lying on his back among the rough grass, an arrow still protruding from his side. He was a young man, and must have been wearing his armour for the first time, for it was still newly burnished from the smith's forge. He said, 'Pull out my sword and place it where I can roll on to it, for I am past all help.'

The boys looked at each other in doubt; yet each knew that to deprive the man of his last wish would be to bring dishonour upon him. Besides, the band of rogues from the shore might pass this way shortly and cause the dying soldier distress by stripping him of his armour and neckring while he was still conscious.

Gwydion shrugged his shoulders and drew out the sword for the Celt. As the boy knelt beside him, it occurred to him to ask where the battle was. With difficulty the man told him that Aulus Plautius was attacking Mai Dun, a fortified earthworks about thirty miles distant. He gasped that the Romans were working their way westwards, on the track of the king Caratacus, who had fled after Camulodunum.

Gwydion asked how the battle went, and the warrior whispered that the Romans were too strong in numbers for the defenders, though they had brought no siege engines with them and relied mainly on infantry. He said that Caratacus had left the fortress as soon as the battle began to go against the Belgae, and had ridden towards the north. But he could speak no more when Gaius tried to press him with questions about the Roman force. Reluctantly, the boys wedged the sword for him with two stones, and after stroking the still-grazing steed, made their way back to the road. When they looked towards the warrior again, he was lying still, his arms spread out, and his head thrown back.

They did not speak for many minutes, and when they did it was to wonder what would happen to the horse. 'He could not have borne us in his present state,' said Gwydion. 'Let us hope that he will graze on the other side of the hill when that band from the shore pass this way.'

So they walked in the direction of Mai Dun, for Gaius was now almost certain that there they would find his father.

6 · After the Battle

By nightfall, foot-sore and hungry, the boys halted on the moorland path which they had followed for most of the day, to see a red glow flickering in the sky. The sullen orange-red hues were reflected from the underside of dark clouds which seemed to stretch over that part of the countryside, making the early evening ominous, almost frightening. Gwydion said grimly, 'We do not need to ask the direction of Mai Dun now. That is the last of the fortress, and of the village at its foot.'

Gaius said, 'Have my people, the Romans, done this, do you think?'

Gwydion shook his head. 'It might just as easily have been the Belgae. They would not leave a fortress whole if they left it; which means that either way, we have been defeated.'

Gaius put his hand on his friend's arm as though to show that among friends there is no such thing as nationality or race. Gwydion smiled back at him, though a little sadly, and thought that if all Celts and Romans were like this, war would be impossible between them.

Then stumbling now, from fatigue and the roughness of the road, they began their melancholy journey towards the burning stronghold, wondering what they might find when at last they reached the place of battle.

The moon was high, when they reached the ruined earthworks, and shone down eerily upon tumbled men and horses who lay here and there upon the ground, throwing a gentle silver light upon this sad carnage, picking out here a raised hand, there a broken helmet; throwing a malicious illumination over things which seemed to cry out for secrecy and peace. High on the summit of the hill, the ruined fortress occasionallly threw up a transient glow of light, as some last beam or stretch of thatch caught fire, and burned itself to an ember. The battle was over, and now across the broad and undulating field, men and even women were moving slowly, some of them carrying torches, seeking their dead, or tearing off the finery of those who were helpless to resist them.

Of the Romans or the Belgae, there were no signs now. It seemed that the tide of battle had swept on, and that the field of Mai Dun was already forgotten history.

The boys looked at each other in despair, for they knew now that their quest was a forlorn one. Gaius' father, if he still lived, might be far away by now, with his infantry, pursuing the enemy westwards, ever westwards. Then, as the two stood silent, unsure what they must now do, an old woman to their right called out to her ragged companions, 'Come! Come! Bring the knife! This Roman dog still breathes!'

Gaius turned in a flash and ran towards the wizened creature who held her torch low so that her friends might do their evil work. He was upon them almost before they saw him, snatching the torch from the hag and bending low over the body. Gwydion, running to join him, his knife already out, saw his friend drop the torch and take the still body in his arms. Then the group of peasants closed in on the Roman boy, and Gwydion charged them, shouting 'Belgae! Caratacus!' They were old people, such as are afraid to venture out until darkness adds its protection to their wickedness, and they were taken aback by this unexpected attack. As they fell away from Gwydion, his friend looked up and said, 'Praise to the gods! It is a Roman, and alive!'

'Stand back!' cried Gwydion to the group of people who moved about him in the shadows. 'If you come nearer, you must taste the edge of this!' He thrust towards them with his knife, and they backed from him. Then the old woman spoke up for the others: 'Young lord,' she said, 'we are poor folk. Our houses have been fired by these Romans. Are we to have no recompense? We found the Roman soldier here; his armour and arm-rings are ours.'

Gwydion would have given them more than they asked for, in his mood of that moment, for his anger was roused that his own people should be so callous towards suffering. He did not know that this stripping of the bodies always happened, as a matter of course, after a battle, that such people as these shivering wretches in their rags regarded it as their right to filch from the dying and the dead whatever they could lay their hands on. Gwydion, a true Celt of the warrior caste, only knew battle as something fine, and noble, and full of heroism.

But Gaius was more practical. All his life he had lived among soldiers, professional Roman legionaries, who were hardened to the other side of war – the tough, mercenary side, in which a man fought for what he might get out of it, and not the honour and the glory of it. Gaius said, 'Here you are, you scavengers! This is his arm-ring; here is his breastplate; and his helmet lies at your feet if you will only take the trouble to bend and pick it up!' He spoke these words with a sneer, and then bent back over the soldier.

The old rag-pickers of the battlefields took the things he offered and, mumbling and cursing, moved away to search the heaps of the slain for other prizes.

When they had gone, Gwydion put up his knife and joined his friend, who bent over the Roman, a javelin-man of one of the crack cohorts by the ribbons that hung pathetically from his shoulders. He had been cruelly wounded by sword-cuts and shook his head, groaning, when they tried to raise him.

'Leave me,' he whispered painfully, 'I have my reward and expected no other. I have a mind to die in peace now, without being disturbed.'

His head fell back and he seemed to lose all interest

in the boys. They stood now, staring down at him, wondering what they should do next, when the man's eyes flickered slowly and opened once more. He seemed to be surprised that they were still with him.

'Go,' he said weakly, 'you will find others more worthy of your aid than I am. Officers and centurions, men of true valour.'

Gaius could not resist the question now. 'Do you know Gracchus, Gracchus the centurion, my friend?' he said anxiously. 'Is he on this field, think you?'

The soldier turned away his head, a bitter smile on his lips. 'There are many called Gracchus, many who are centurions, it seems, to a common soldier. I do not know. Search near the hillside if you would find the honourable dead.'

Then the man gave a great sigh and rolled on to his side and Gaius saw his friend's lips moving and knew that he was saying the Celtic parting-words for one who was now going on a long journey. They covered the soldier with his cloak and began to pick their way towards the hill, silent and bewildered.

At last Gaius said, 'It is impossible for us to search this field. By daylight we might stand a chance of finding a man, but by night and in this confusion we are doomed to failure.'

Gwydion put his hand on his friend's arm. 'We must search, friend,' he said. 'If your father is here, he will need what help we can give him without delay; and if he is not here, then we shall know that he is either safe in Camulodunum or that he has passed on with the others towards the west, unharmed.'

Now they were at the foot of the hill, where the going was made more difficult by the tumbled mounds of the lower earthworks. Here and there lay such debris as a battle would produce: the wheels of a smashed chariot, the broken totem-poles of a defeated tribe, the bodies of horses, killed either by the arrows of the enemy or pole-axed by their charioteers when they fell, entangled in their harness, in the mad rush from the approaching legions.

Suddenly Gwydion gave a shout, 'Look, over there,' he cried. 'A Roman Eagle still standing! We must search there!' Then he began to run, stumbling in the half-light over tussocky turf and obstacles of war, closely followed by Gaius, who did not dare to hope that they might discover his father.

Between two earthen ridges, where a gaunt ash tree bowed down low over the little enclosure, the two boys saw the great bulk of a Roman field-wagon, tilted almost on to its side, its axles broken by the great weight that it carried. It was an ammunition cart, laden with supplies of sling-shot, iron bars, for making horse-shoes, even the small portable furnaces that the Roman smiths needed for forging arrow-heads or re-tempering swords.

Above all the scattered armaments that lay piled near the wrecked wagon, an eagle standard rose, catching the moonlight on its bright surfaces.

'They must have made a stand here,' said Gaius as he ran on towards it. 'Only a man of some authority would be in charge of such a wagon.'

Then Gwydion had raced on past him again and was already clambering over the tumbled sacks and bundles of iron. Yet what he saw caused him to halt, half-afraid, and to wait until his friend had come up with him. 'They have made a gallant stand,' he said, gazing down at the men who lay about the bright standard. 'But I dare not go down among them to look.'

Gaius did not seem to hear him, but pushed by him and bent in the shadows, working as gently as he could, like a creature possessed but hating the task which he had to perform.

Gwydion half-turned away, by now sickened by the carnage of this battlefield, all hope gone from him. Then suddenly he heard his friend give a great gasp, of mingled amazement and gratitude, it seemed. Gwydion turned again hardly daring to look, and then he, too, slithered into the ditch to be beside his friend.

Gaius looked up tearfully. 'He lay beneath them all, at the very foot of the standard,' he said. 'He must have fallen facing the first onrush down the hill.'

Gwydion did not speak. There was nothing he could have said that would have let him express his thankfulness at this almost incredible piece of good fortune. Then a great fear struck him.

'Is he . . . ?' he began to say, hardly bearing to look at his friend's shining face. But the question was unnecessary, for the centurion's hand moved, as though he were even then waving on his forward troops into battle, and the boys heard him speak, faintly but still with the unmistakable tones of authority.

'Keep down, you in the first rank! This is no

game of hide-and-seek! These tribesmen carry edged weapons!'

There was something in the centurion's spirit that seemed indestructible, and suddenly Gwydion found himself weeping with pleasure as he clasped the cold hand of this soldier of Rome.

Gaius smiled across at his friend, understanding the emotions which so moved the Celt.

'You must be proud of such a father,' said Gwydion.

'I thank the gods for letting us find him again,' said the young Roman. 'And for giving me a comrade like you,' he added, but under his breath, for his education had been based on Spartan precepts, which taught that it was unmanly to make any show of the emotions.

Gwydion looked away for a second or two, suddenly remembering that day above Camulodunum when his own father's chariot tilted before the charging legions. Then, shaking the water from his eyes, he smiled and with a typical Celtic bravado, punched Gaius lightly in the chest.

It was a blow which carried more love in it than any caress. It was also an expression of the boy's relief that, so unexpectedly, they had found Gracchus again. At least this was something salvaged from the ruinous chaos that now seemed to be sweeping across Britain.

7 · The Beehive Hut

The centurion lay still now. There was a long, deep wound across one temple which must have come from a javelin thrust or a sling-shot. His right leg lay twisted beneath him and had every appearance of being broken. But, as far as the boys could tell, he was not gravely wounded; that is, if they could get him away to warmth and comfort before he caught a chill in the night air and took a fever.

Now Gwydion began to run here and there among the debris of the field, searching for something which might act as a stretcher. He returned at last with the broken shafts of two banners and a cloak or two. He had also found various pieces of clothing, a tunic and a pair of brightly-coloured Celtic breeches, together with a belt. They had been lying in a heap, he said, as though foragers had collected them for future disposal but had left them temporarily.

So together the boys wrapped up the unconscious soldier as best they could, and tied the cloaks about the flag-staffs to make a stretcher. As they rolled the wounded man on to this, he groaned and called out for his son. Gaius stroked his hand and told him that he was there, though it was apparent that the man did not understand what was said, for he continued to speak of Gaius as though he was not there.

At last the boys began their slow march away from the grim battlefield of Mai Dun, bearing well to the east at first, in case later bands of armed men should visit the place of slaughter and discover them. By now both Gaius and Gwydion were almost exhausted with hunger and the long journey of the day. They had had little to eat and only spring water to drink; but there was no time now to think of that, and they staggered on under their heavy load, with each step putting a little more distance between the nightmare field and themselves.

At the dead of night, they turned off their course into a small wood, and rested for a while in a moonlit glade. They moved on, however, when a skin-clad herdsman looked at them round a tree, threatening them with an ancient spear and shouting at them in a language that even Gwydion found it difficult to understand.

After that, they trudged on and on almost till dawn broke, and at last, in a little valley, came upon a solitary house, in the old beehive shape, nestling in the shadow of a clump of pine-trees. From the carefully-tended fields about this house, it seemed that its owner was a hardworking, respectable person. As they drew nearer, a black-and-white shepherd dog ran out towards them, wagging his long tail and baring his teeth at the same time. The dog stopped a few yards away from them, and began to growl. Gwydion drew his knife, resting one shaft of the stretcher on his raised thigh, and threatened the dog; but this only made it bark more angrily. Gaius said, 'It is useless; this is a faithful beast, and it would be wrong to harm him. We must wait.'

They set the stretcher down on the hillside and sat down in the damp grass of dawn, while the dog circled them, sniffing and barking at every step or so. At last a man came out of the hovel, carrying a billhook in his hand, and peering up the hill, shading his eyes with his hand. He whistled to the dog, which dropped its tail and ran back to him, belly close to the ground. Then he shouted, 'Throw away your weapons and come down here. There is food for you if you come in peace.'

He was a big man, but quite old. He wore a soft leather cap which dangled about one ear, and a loose gown of grey wool that reached down to his knees. Below this, the boys saw his wide Celtic trousers, brightly patterned in squares of red and yellow, held in tight at the ankle by leathern thongs.

Gwydion said, 'This is a man of the Durotriges. They are mainly farming folk, herdsmen, and do not go into battle often – though they are stout to defend what they call their rights. This one will be good to us if we do not try to trick him.'

The boys walked down towards him with their hands wide apart, so that he could see their weaponless state. He lowered his billhook as they approached and said, 'Who is that who lies up the hill on the stretcher?'

Gaius said, 'It is my father, sadly wounded at Mai Dun.'

The old man gazed up the hill, seeing the tartan that covered the body. 'There is always room in my house for a good Celt,' he said. 'Bring him down. He will die of cold up there, for the sun has yet to warm the air.'

He paid no more attention to them, but turned and went into his house. When the boys returned with the

centurion, there was a blazing fire in the middle of the
earthen floor, and steam already rising from the metal
pot which swung on a tripod above it.

When they had eaten and had forced some nourish-
ment into the throat of the Roman, Gaius stood up and
said simply, 'Master, I am a Roman and this is my
father. I have no wish to deceive you. If you tell us
that we must leave your house, we shall go, as soon as
my father is warmed; and we shall thank you forever
in our prayers for your kindness.'

The old man lay beside the fire stroking the dog,
which was now quite docile, and seemed to have taken
to the visitors. He drank from his horn-cup without
looking at the boy and said, just as simply, 'It was
wrong of you to wrap your father in the tartan of the
enemy, for that is deceit, and a man should be prepared
to face the world without such tricks. But you are a
young man of truth, I can hear that in your straight
speech, and such folk are not many in the world today.
I say to you, that whether you be Roman or Celt, it
matters not, provided you act fairly with me. I serve
no lord here; I am my own master. I shall not run off
to tell anyone that you are here. You may stay until
you wish to go. If you are handy lads in the field, or
at keeping an eye on the sheep, then I shall count it
a blessing that you came this way. As for the man, I
have some skill in herbs and cures, and what I can do,
that I shall.'

Gaius held out his hand to the old man, who took it,
smiling that a mere boy should behave in such an adult
manner.

'Now sit you down again,' he said, 'and drink another cup of this hot broth, while I look at the man and see what injuries he has gathered.'

So, after many weary miles, the boys found a home, and Gaius and his father were reunited.

Part Three

1 · Who Dares Pick Herbs?

Gracchus, the centurion, recovered but slowly. The wound in his temple healed within a few weeks, but his broken right leg took months to knit properly, and it was spring again before he could walk without pain. At first, overjoyed that his son had found him, he did not wish for any other company than Gaius, and Gwydion often wept in the dark to think that Gaius had a father, but that his own was gone for ever. But later the centurion took to the Belgic boy once more, and often said how glad he was that he had treated him well after Camulodunum, for Gwydion had been the real reason for finding him on the battlefield. Gaius would never have left Lugdunum, had it not been for his friend.

The old farmer acted with great kindness towards them all, and seemed to enjoy having them in the hut, for he was a lonely man, he told them, since his daughter had gone away to be married among the Silures.

The boys helped him as much as they could, with the ploughing and the sowing and in tending the hives and watching the sheep and goats. While they were busy on his behalf, he would sit in the hut with Gracchus, talking, or would walk slowly about the hillside with him, supporting him by the arm when his leg became tired or stiff.

Gracchus said one night, 'My army passed on and left me for dead. I am no doubt crossed off their list now, for they imagine me to be sleeping the long sleep on the field of Mai Dun. It is a great temptation to let them go on thinking that. It would suit me to stay here, and build another such house on the next hill. I have a hankering after a quiet life! I would not even regret leaving the house in Lugdunum, and the pension I am entitled to from Rome!'

Gaius gazed at him in joy. 'I would like that too, father,' he said. 'This is a place where a man could be happy.'

Gracchus nodded thoughtfully. 'Yes,' he said, 'an ordinary man – but not a Roman soldier; not a centurion, my lad. For a soldier still has his duty to do, even though his friends have given him up for dead. My training in the Legion has been too long for me to forget it. I must put aside my dream of becoming a quiet Celtic farmer, and as soon as I can, I must report back to the Legion.'

The boys looked at him in disappointment. The old man shrugged his shoulders and went out to milk the cow. 'A man must do as he must,' he said, as though he felt that Gracchus was foolish, nevertheless.

Later that evening, when they were all seated about the fire again, their hunger appeased by the old man's honey-cakes and good strong cheese, the centurion said, 'Where is the Roman army now, my friend?'

The old man said, 'Only the young men, who ride about the land, know truly where they are. I have lost touch with such affairs, for the Romans would not trouble me in my little hut here. I should not bother to hide even if the beacon were lit on yonder hill, as it is in times of danger. I can only guess where they might be. From my daughter, who lives among the Silures, across the big river, many weeks' journey away, I know that Caratacus has set up his new kingdom in Siluria, and has gathered together a great warband there. Now, it stands to reason that the Romans, having defeated him in the East, will not permit him to become a great danger to them in the West. So, it is my belief that the Romans may try to crush him there. It is my advice, therefore, that he who wishes to find a Roman Legion had best make his way to Siluria, either now, or in a short while; for there they must surely be.'

Gracchus nodded and thought over this news, his pale face grave. Gwydion sat in a dark corner of the hut, also thinking about the old man's words, for he knew that where Caratacus was, there would his mother be, and with his mother, as the report had said, would be Math – his old, true, trusted friend, Math. Gwydion determined that, whatever Gaius and his father did, he would set off to the great river one day soon.

The same idea had come to Gracchus, who now stared through the firelight at the young Belgic boy, wondering whether he would wish to accompany them, for the centurion no longer regarded him as a slave, but as a free person who had a right to choose where and with whom he would travel, if at all. He wondered how he could broach the matter to Gwydion; but, as the fates had it, the matter was taken out of his hands, quite without warning, a few days later, when Gracchus and the two boys were walking in the shallow valleys, looking for roots and herbs to add to the old farmer's medicine store.

2 · Young Warrior on a Horse

The sun was hardly at its height when Gwydion looked up and gazed with consternation along the hilltop. A long line of horsemen, about a score of them, was moving above them, dark against the sunny sky. At first he thought of calling to Gracchus and Gaius to hide, for they were plucking herbs at the edge of a little green spinney, and might escape notice. Then they heard a sharp cry from the hilltop, and Gwydion saw that it was too late. The horsemen came swooping down the slope towards them, waving lances and long barbarian swords, their red woollen cloaks swinging out behind them in the morning breeze.

As they drew nearer, Gwydion saw that they were not Belgae. Each man wore a round helmet of leather, decorated with feathers or with dangling strings of blue beads, and dark green trousers, strapped with leather from thigh to ankle, and supported by a broad leathern belt. They wore the upper body bare, their dark skin crossed with streaks of woad, and tattooed on breast and waist with long whitish scars, made with knife-sharp tattoo sticks. Gwydion observed that one or two of them wore short sticks of bone thrust through the ear-lobes as decorations. It was this that gave Gwydion the answer to the problem – they must be Silurians, a wandering band of foragers, perhaps the comitatus of some Silurian prince, spending the time from seed-strewing to harvest in ranging the country to steal what they could.

Then he had no more time to speculate on these horsemen, for they surrounded the three herb-pickers, riding round and round them until they were quite dizzy at watching the fast ponies and their bright, dangling harness. Then suddenly there was a shout, and the circling stopped; their leader broke from the ring and rode towards Gwydion, smiling, his long sword held loosely across his thighs, his black hair blowing across his painted face.

'Gwydion! As sure as the gods live in oak-trees!' he said.

Gwydion stared at him in wonder, then he ran to meet the other as he swung from the high sheepskin saddle. 'Math, by all the wonders of the stones!' he yelled. 'What good fortune! Oh, Math!'

The centurion and his son stood in amazement as the two hugged each other, and almost did a dance of pleasure at meeting so unexpectedly that bright morning. The other warriors sat upright on their horses, straight-faced and unsmiling, waiting only for the signal to ride on, or to cut down these three, whichever their leader ordered.

Gwydion held Math at arm's length; 'But Math,' he cried, 'What are you doing, dressed like this?' Then, for a moment, a small shadow passed across the Silure's face, but it was gone in a flash and he was smiling once

more. 'Did I never tell you, friend,' he said, 'I am a prince among my own folk!'

Gwydion stopped smiling, for he had read Math's unspoken thoughts. Math had been about to say – 'and not your slave any longer.' Then Gwydion half-turned to the Romans and was about to introduce them to Math, but there was something in Gracchus's eyes which forbade him. Instead, he said, 'These are two dear friends of mine.'

Math stared at them insolently; it was apparent that he did not recognize the centurion, who now wore Celtic clothes and had perforce grown a short beard while he had been ill and could not be shaven. Besides, without his Roman helmet, he looked a different man. Nor would Math know Gaius. At last he bowed very stiffly to them and said that Gwydion's friends were his friends; though from the way in which he said this, Gwydion was not sure that he meant it. Indeed, he felt that a great change had come over his old friend in the year that had separated them.

At last one of the horsemen rode up and spoke to Math, pointing to the sun, indicating that they must not delay. Math spoke back to him so roughly that for a moment Gwydion was afraid that they might come to blows. Instead the man bowed his head, and went back to his place, to wait silently until the young leader should decide to mount again.

Math said to Gwydion, 'Now that I have found you, I cannot let you go again. You must come with us.'

Gwydion looked at the Romans, and could see that Gracchus did not wish to accompany this party. But Math glared at him and signed to one of his men, who rode just behind the centurion and drew his long sword. Then Gwydion realized that although no word had been said, they were in truth prisoners. He made himself smile at Math, and vowed inwardly that as soon as he got the chance he would give his former slave a piece of his mind for this manner of behaviour.

Yet it soon became apparent that Math was interested only in Gwydion; he regarded the other two as being worthless, necessary encumbrances who could not be left behind lest they spread the news of his whereabouts. He would not even give them permission to return to the hut and wish the old man goodbye. This angered

Gwydion, who rode behind Math on the strong pony, but he realized that now his friend was the powerful one, and if anything, their former positions were reversed. Gwydion was now the slave, when it came to obeying orders!

He turned once and winked to Gracchus and the lad, just to let them see that he was still their friend, and then the party set off northwards towards Siluria.

Gracchus and his son were made to march much of the way, in spite of Gwydion's protests; though the centurion would not allow the Belgic boy to say that he had but recently broken a leg, for, he whispered, a Roman must never beg for mercy.

Sometimes Math was very cross when the Romans could not walk faster, and said that they were delaying the band. Nor would he allow Gwydion to let the centurion change places and ride on the pony.

On such occasions, Gwydion often felt like asking Math what had come over him that he should be so changed, yet it came out one night as they all lay round a camp-fire, eating greedily from the carcass of a red deer which one of the men had run down. Math said, 'I shall never forget the Roman camp, Gwydion. When they had taken you away, I was sure they were going to torture you, or kill you. I was frantic with suffering and fear, yes, I will admit it, fear! Then, before dawn while I was still waiting for my turn to come, I found a knife that someone had carelessly left near the tent. It must have been dropped in the battle and overlooked. I cut the bonds of all the prisoners who could walk. Two of those with broken legs made me cut their throats. Then we slashed a hole in the tent, stabbed the sleeping guard, and ran.'

Gracchus listened to this with horror; Gwydion felt that he must tell Math who had left the knife, but a look in the centurion's eyes once more made him stop.

Math prattled on gaily, saying that from that moment he had become a new person; he had remembered his destiny as a prince, and had ceased to be a slave. Now he knew that, unaided, he could kill men, could defy the Romans. 'So,' he ended, 'you see me as I am, my true self.' But now Gwydion was not sure whether he liked this new Math. He spoke secretly to Gracchus when the others were asleep that night, asking the man what they must do. The centurion smiled grimly and said, 'Your course is plotted for you. You must go to your mother, whatever happens. But we are different. This young prince means us harm, I can sense it. We shall escape, if the chance arises, and make our way back to the Legion. No, do not protest, Gwydion, you may wake one of them. Just carry on as ever, and do not be surprised if you awake one morning to find that we have done what I say. Remember that our good wishes are always with you, and one day we may even meet again, and be friends as we have been in the past.'

In the dying firelight, they shook hands, the young boy and the gnarled old veteran. Then they wrapped their blankets about them and tried to sleep, under the bright stars, with the chill wind of late spring blowing over them from the broad river that lay a mile or two to their left hands.

Now the distance to Siluria was small, and if the

Romans were to escape, they must do it quickly, for in three days at the most, the war band would be knocking on the gates of Caratacus's fortress.

3 · Pirates in the River!

Sadly for Gracchus, the watchful comitatus of Math gave him no opportunity of slipping away unobserved before the party reached Siluria. Those blue-stained horsemen had eyes like hawks, and always rode as though ready, at the next beat of their horses' hooves, to defend themselves against a hidden enemy, or to attack some unsuspecting prey, some careless warrior or sleeping Roman, at the next bend.

Once, in the still hours of the night, Gwydion persuaded the centurion to write a word or two for Gryf – though the boy hardly knew how such a message might ever be transmitted to Gaul; and once, as Gwydion ran alongside Math's pony, holding the stirrup, well ahead of the rest of the band, he said to his old friend, 'Math, I find a change in you.' The other had looked down from the saddle, with veiled eyes, smiling faintly and sarcastically, 'Say on, dear friend,' he had answered.

Gwydion said, daring everything at one throw, 'You are not the person I knew, the person I used to like. You are different – callous, hard, and arrogant.'

Math rode on for a while before replying, and when he did, his voice was strong and serious. 'Then I was a slave,' he said. 'Now I am myself again, a prince. A prince cannot walk the world barefooted; nor can he show mercy to every fool he meets along the way. I accept you again, my Gwydion, because in your fashion you were kind to me when I was a prisoner in your father's house. I lack many qualities, but I do not lack loyalty. I never forget, Gwydion – no, not even the things you sometimes said to me when you remembered that you were the son of the house, and I the slave.'

Then Gwydion was so depressed that, had his mother not been living in the court of Caratacus, he would have thrown in his lot with Gracchus and Gaius, and have tried to break away at the first chance.

After that he did not attempt to talk to Math, and the last stages of the journey were oppressive with a heaviness that Gwydion had never experienced before.

Then, it was too late to think of these things, for the guard at the stockade let them through and blew three loud blasts on the bull's horn which served him as a trumpet, to announce their approach. Men ran out and prostrated themselves before the young lord, Math, and led away the horses of the party, staring boldly and in-sultingly at the three new arrivals, as though they were slaves of the lowest order, and hardly to be considered as human creatures. Gwydion noticed that all the menial work within the stockade was done by dark-skinned Silurians and not by fair-haired Belgae. This gave him some hope, for he felt that Caratacus had al-ready asserted his mastery over this earlier hill-folk, and that the king's kindness would soon replace the sullen malice of the prince, Math.

It was with pleasure, even, that Gwydion found himself being pushed behind Math, into the great thatched hall of the king. The air was thick with smoke from the great central fire, and it was difficult to see at first; but Gwydion scanned the hall for the sight of his mother. He saw that there were no women present, and his heart sank.

Many men thronged the hall, standing three or four deep round its walls; while at the far end, the king sat in a high carved chair, surrounded by tall fair-skinned Belgae, his personal bodyguard. Math stood before Gwydion, facing the king across the long extent of hard earthen floor. Two of the bodyguard put horns to their lips and blew a long wailing blast, and Math, his right hand stretched up and out, in something like the Roman salute, walked forward towards Caratacus. Just before he began his march he half-turned and whispered to Gwydion, 'Stay there, until you are called.'

Gwydion looked round for Gaius and his father, and saw that they were held by the arms, almost in the doorway, like prisoners. He saw that they stared indignantly at the Belgic king, and knew that this meeting might well turn out badly for one or the other.

He turned back and looked at Caratacus. He seemed to have aged in the short year since Gwydion had spied on him in the Council Hall of Camulodunum. He lolled, rather than sat, in his carven chair, his big body slack, his hands white and fat; Gwydion noticed that his hair was almost grey, though it had shone like spun-gold as he stood gallant in his chariot to take the Roman arrows. Now, in place of that bull-helmet, he wore a narrow circlet of gold about his brow, and a long toga-like purple robe of linen, that covered his feet. He was more like a dissolute Roman consul than a king. Now that fine aquiline nose was pinched and cruel as an eagle's beak; that mobile, humorous mouth had taken on the shape of petulant pride.

Gwydion turned his eyes to Math, who walked straight to the king, hand upraised. When the boy was within a few feet of the chair, Caratacus raised his hand too, so that they touched, palm to palm, and stayed in that position for the space of three. Then Math knelt before him, and at last stood at his side, turning to point towards Gwydion.

'That is my friend, Gwydion of the Belgae,' he said, so that all could hear, 'Gwydion, whose father was your henchman, Caradoc; Gwydion who treated me well when I was a slave in his house.'

Caratacus smiled the length of the hall, ironically, as though he no longer trusted anyone, as though he no longer wished to be reminded of those whom he had known in that other life, before the Romans came. He said, slowly and indolently, 'Yes, Gwydion! His mother will doubtless be pleased to see him again. Tell him that he may go to her later this evening, when the audience is over.'

He did not call Gwydion to him, nor did he seem to notice his existence any further, but turned towards Math and began to ask him about his hunting-trip, what quarry they had raised, what weather they had had, whether he had got as far as Mai Dun, and whether there were any pickings left there for lively riders.

Math answered him quietly, but respectfully, and

was then waved to a stool set at the king's right knee, where he sat, a puppet prince beside his powerful master.

A tall Belgic chieftain brought a horn of wine for the boy, but handed it to him in such a way that it spilled over his tartan trousers. Gwydion noticed that Math's face did not change; he noticed also that the chieftain smiled as he did it, a smile which was reflected on the faces of the other Belgae who surrounded the throne. Gwydion sensed now that Math held his position against the wishes of the warrior chieftains who had accompanied Caratacus into exile, and in a way felt a slight twinge of sympathy for the lad, who, caught in the millstones of a country's chaos, was forced to act as he was bidden. Indeed, Gwydion speculated, Math is still as much of a slave as he has ever been.

How long this sad farce might have dragged on, Gwydion could not tell, but suddenly he heard voices behind him, the voices of Gracchus arguing with his captors. The Roman's voice was grave and undershot with the note of anger, though an anger which he knew well enough how to keep under control.

Caratacus looked up, from making some pleasantry with the yellow-haired spearman at his left side, and said loudly to Math, 'Who are these other friends of yours, that they should think fit to break the king's silence in the king's hall? Are they too Belgae, dear Math?'

Now, Gwydion's heart beat fast, for the lives of his friends hung on the answer which Math should give. Both Gracchus and Gaius were clothed, Celtic fashion,

in tunic and trews, and both now wore their hair long
and plaited, Belgic style. Both spoke a form of Celtic, almost as a second language, for neither had known a
time when there were not Celtic servants, or soldiers, or
friends, in the house or in the Legion, with whom they
must speak every day. Math had never inquired about
them, not even once, during the ride to Siluria, and
Gwydion had ventured no remarks about their true
identity. He had taken it that Math considered them
Celts with whom he had travelled from Gaul. Now, his
heart beat for he waited for Math to say that these were
Celtic friends of Gwydion. But Math looked them in
the eye and said, 'When the king demands, I answer
with truth.' Caratacus whispered hoarsely and even
menacingly, 'That is wise, Math, for my pride would
not stomach a lie; no, not from my very mother herself.'

Math's face twisted with some emotion which Gwydion could not understand then, because of the beating
of his heart; but he saw the boy rise from his stool and
point towards Gracchus, and heard him say, as from a
great, deathly distance, 'My lord, that is the Roman
centurion who came to take Gwydion away after the
affair at Camulodunum. The other, the boy, I do not
know, though I believe him to be a Roman also.'

Caratacus pushed Math aside back to his stool, and
held up his hand towards the guards at the door. Gwydion heard a sudden scuffle behind him, and swung
round, to see Gracchus and Gaius fighting with a knot
of Silurians who were trying to bind them.

Gwydion made a step towards the group when two
guards ran out and pinioned his arms to his side,

roughly. He kicked with all his force, but one of the men twisted his arm so viciously behind his back that he fell to the floor, and so did not see the end of the struggle at the door. When at last they allowed him to rise, the centurion and his son were nowhere to be seen. The hall was full of laughter and ribald comment as Gwydion stood again, a warrior on each side of him, to face the king. Caratacus regarded him, smiling, for a long while, and then said, as to Math, 'This boy's father was my trusted henchman. The son has given himself to Rome, it appears. What cure is there for such a disease, think you, Math?'

Math stood up and seemed about to kneel before the king. 'Gwydion acted in a moment of hot blood, my lord,' he said. 'He is tired and should be forgiven.'

Caratacus said, 'Once the poison has entered the body, a man is never free of it.'

Math flung himself now before the Belgic king, but Gwydion strained forward, shouting, 'Get up, Math, you fool! I will not have you abasing yourself for me. Caratacus could trust my father, and I am my father's son. That should be good enough for him!'

At this there was a great outcry in the hall, but one chiefly of laughter from the assembled Silurians, though the Belgae about the chair looked angry, and even turned to cast threatening glances at their dark-skinned allies who leaned against the thatched walls.

Then Caratacus began to laugh too, his old laugh, the sound which Gwydion had heard him make when the meadhorn had passed freely at a feast, or when he had ridden up to their door to call for a cup of wine after a hard day's hunting, and had listened to some dry story that Gwydion's father had come out to tell him. Gwydion looked at the king in surprise, wondering what this sudden change might betoken. But the king's face was open and amused. He called out the length of the hall,

'Well said, young cock of the tribes! There spoke the true Belgic heart of you! Come here, Gwydion, son of Caswallawn, and take the oath your father took! Come now, while the sun shines in my heart!'

He settled himself in his chair and held out his hands. Gwydion felt himself torn between two ideals; that of fealty to his liege-lord, and that of faithfulness to his two good Roman friends. Even as he walked forward, in confusion, however, his quick brain told him that he could best serve his Roman friends by making himself a friend of Caratacus. There was no way out, indeed. And so Gwydion at last knelt before the king and placed his hands within the king's jewelled hands. He looked up once to see that the king's sharp eyes were boring into his own, boring down to his heart, searching for any treachery that might be hidden there. Caratacus may have got fat and soft in his habits since his defeat, but his old shrewdness was still there, as sharp and as strong as ever, like a well-tempered sword, which, though it has lain for many months in a stream, is still a deadly weapon, despite its rust.

Gwydion looked down in misery. This was not the manner in which he had once dreamed to take the oath of service. Then the king's voice began to say the words which the boy was to repeat after him. Gwydion heard the first phrase and was about to say them again when just outside the door a shrill horn blew, urgently, distractedly, not to be denied. Then a great shout went up from the stockade, 'Pirates in the river! The Irish pirates are coming in two longboats!'

Horses began to neigh outside, and the men in the hall placed their hands upon their swords, as though to be sure that they were ready as soon as the king should command them to move.

Gwydion looked up at Caratacus; the king was staring over his head, into the distance, forgetful now of oaths and loyalty, his old warrior-flame enkindled by this sudden offer of battle.

Gwydion felt the king's hands go slack about his, and at last drop them. The king rose and said softly, 'This can wait, Gwydion! There will be other times for you to ride with me. Go to your mother, and tell her the news of your long journey.'

Then the king was striding down the hall, his long robe swaying with the steps he made, giving him the appearance of a priest, a druid, rather than a warrior-king.

Gwydion looked up to see that Math was signalling to the Silurians about the wall, ordering them to follow him. Gwydion rose, but Math waved him aside. 'This is a battle which I must fight with my own folk,' he said. 'Your place is in the bower, until he has taken your oath.' So the men filed out of the hall, leaving Gwydion almost alone, save for an old man who crooned in a corner of long-forgotten wars.

4 · The Silencing of Math!

In her bower, Gwydion's mother had finished weeping over his safe return. She sat beside him, gazing at him as though she had never seen him before; grasping his hands as though she would never let him leave again. Then slowly and sadly she spoke to him of the change that had come over Caratacus.

'He is a bitter, disappointed man, my son,' she said. 'If your father were alive now, he would love the king no longer.'

And she told him of poor Math, who was little more than a doll, to dance as Caratacus willed; Math, who was the prince in his own right over Siluria, but whom Caratacus had taken as his ward, since Math had once been a slave among the Belgae.

'When Caratacus has got all he can from the boy, there will be no more Math, Gwydion,' she said. 'Then Caratacus will be the undisputed king of this country. He has lost one kingdom, but has now found another.'

Gwydion said, 'But will not Math's own people fight for him, mother?'

She smiled sadly and said,' Gwydion, you know little of the world's ways, even though you have travelled to Lugdunum and back! No, these Silurians are a beaten people, beaten already in their own hearts. They are fit only for midnight raids, or for foraging in small war-bands, attacking defenceless folk on lonely farms, or in woodland glades. They are an ancient people who had never known anything but new conquerors coming, wave after wave of them, defeat after defeat. All they want is a strong master to make them do as he tells them. They are like dogs, lazy if they are left alone, dangerous if they are set on by a cruel master. Math is not their master, though some of them, his war-band, I think, still remember his old father, and have sworn to follow him. But should the occasion arise, I think that even his war-band, his comitatus, would desert him in favour of our king.'

She spoke the last words with such bitterness that Gwydion had to look hard at his mother, to make sure that it was her voice he had heard. He had never heard her speak in this manner before. Then he said, 'Mother, I did not take the oath today. The king went out and left me before I could swear to him.'

The noblewoman smiled and patted his hand. 'Do not let that worry you, my son,' she said. 'I have a feeling that your father would not have wished you to take the oath to this man now. Rest assured, those who are his liege-men will be called on to do many things before long which their honour would not have allowed them to think of, but for their fealty. That is the curse of oath-taking – it causes a man to act against his better judgement and his honour very often.'

Gwydion had never known his mother so cynical, so practical, before. It seemed that his father's death had changed her in many ways. He said, 'The Romans are imprisoned. They were good to me.'

She nodded and replied, 'They were good to me, my son. Your centurion was the means of my travelling here unmolested. Did you know that he had arranged for me to be offered a home for life, as a Roman citizen? What Celt would have done that? None! They are too busy cutting each other's throats, my son, to bother about sad widows after a battle.'

Gwydion said, 'What are we to do? We cannot leave them to rot in the prison. He may even torture them if they do not bow to his will, and I am certain that Gracchus would never bend the knee to him.'

Then Gwydion's mother smiled, the first gay smile that had crossed her gentle face since this conversation had begun.

'They need not bow the knee to him,' she said quietly, nor need you, if you do not wish to.'

His face was so puzzled at these words that she bent towards him and whispered, 'I too have a debt to pay to these Romans. They not only offered me peace, but they gave back my son to me. I shall pay that debt as your father would have done, Romans or not. In a short while you will hear the sound of the screech-owl, repeated three times. That will be a signal, and will mean that one of my servants, an old woman who used to work in the dairy when we were all togther, has done what I have ordered her to do.'

'What is that, mother?' asked Gwydion, breathless with excitement now.

'She will have flung a sharp knife through the window of the hut where the Romans are imprisoned. It is then their task to cut a way out through the weakest part of the thatch and make their escape. There are three fast horses tethered outside the stockade near their prison. It will then be their own affair.'

Gwydion said, 'Three horses, mother? Who is going with them then?'

His mother looked at him searchingly. 'Who but you, my son?' she said. 'You would be breaking no oath, for you have not made one. Go with them, take the oath to their Caesar and try to make a good, orderly world for men to live in.'

She took Gwydion's hand then and he saw that her eyes were filling with tears. 'I could not leave you, mother,' he said.

She smiled at him through her tears. 'My son,' she said, 'let me be a little of the Roman, too. I order you to go this night, if your friends are fortunate enough to cut their way out before the others return. I have waited long enough to see you again, I can wait a little while longer. One day, and perhaps soon, I believe that Rome will make an end of this man, Caratacus; and then we shall be free to live together again, under one roof; free to try and make a new life for ourselves in an ordered world. You must go, so as to make this home for me. Have no fear, I will find you, wherever you are.'

As she said these last words, the cry of the screech-owl sounded close outside the hut. 'Be ready, now,' she whispered. 'Lead them northwards towards the country of Madog of the Ordovices. He is a friend of Rome, I hear, and will give you shelter until you can go to the Roman officer in charge of the new garrison at Vricon.'

Then she felt within her long gown and held something out to her son. 'Take this,' she said. 'It was your father's.'

Gwydion looked down at the object which she held

out to him, glistening in the torchlight. It was his father's ceremonial hunting knife, a splendid long weapon, of hardened iron, its jade handle set with arabesques of beaten gold, its pommel a piece of red coral, carved into the shape of an acorn. It lay there in his hand, glinting viciously in the light; and as he grasped it, a new sensation of power came upon him. Now he felt like the son of his brave father, a son who would not abandon his true friends, who would not bow the knee to any tyrant, of whatever blood he might be.

Gwydion knelt and took up the hem of his mother's gown and put it to his lips in homage. 'Good-bye, dear mother,' he said, 'I shall obey you; and one day when the world is kinder we shall come together in happiness again.'

Then he rose and turned from her, for he feared to look into her face again, lest her tears should dissuade him from his strong, new purpose. He wrapped his cloak about him and walked to the door. But even as his hand went out to open it, the door swung open and Math stood there, his chest rising and falling with exertion, a broad streak of blood across his face and down his neck. In his right hand he carried something which he held by the hair, long red hair, something which still dripped to the wooden floor. Gwydion stared at the severed head, horrified, dumb. Math was the first to speak. 'It was a short fight, Gwydion,' he said. 'I have brought this trophy for my foster-mother. An offering to a brave mother from a warrior-son.'

Gwydion saw the distaste in his gentle mother's face. He was suddenly angry with Math, in a different way from anything he had known before. He said, 'Throw that thing outside, you barbarian!'

Math looked down at him with a sneer across his lips. 'Oho! my friend,' he said, 'are you already so much the Roman that you dare call me barbarian?'

Gwydion knew now that Gracchus and Gaius must have cut their way through the wall. There was no time to lose if he was to ride with them. He decided not to antagonize Math any longer. Instead, he forced himself to smile and made as though to pass through the door.

'Where are you going, Gwydion?' said the other, standing in his path.

Gwydion looked over his shoulder into the night, and saw that already the war-band of Caratacus was returning. The flames of their torches shone here and there on the hillside, approaching swiftly; and the sound of their victory songs came louder and louder across the wall of the stockade. Gwydion said, 'I go to meet Caratacus, friend. Stay and speak with my mother until I return.'

But Math's eyes narrowed. He said, 'Where you go, there will I go too, my Roman friend! I think you might need an escort if you walk abroad this night!'

Math set down the head of the Irish pirate and made to link his arm in Gwydion's. Then the mother spoke, anxiously, almost beseechingly; 'Math, my son,' she said, 'let Gwydion go. Think of your old friendship with him, and let him go, for my sake. I beg it, Math.'

But the young man, fired with his new victory, said to her in a dangerous voice, 'Mother, Caratacus will punish traitors, whoever they may be. I go with Gwydion for the safety of his spirit!'

Now Gwydion saw that this was a hopeless situation, for Math was so far under the domination of the Belgic king that he had brushed aside all other ties. Math must be treated like any enemy, for he was dangerous as one. Gwydion gave him one more chance. 'Math,' he said, 'for the sake of our old friendship, let me go.'

Math turned on him with a grim smile, 'So, there is some trickery afoot!' he said triumphantly, and his hand went down to the bull's horn that slung from his broad belt. Gwydion could afford to waste no time; for now he knew that Math would betray both his mother and himself to Caratacus, in spite of their old comradeship. Gwydion leaned sideways, catching the slighter-built boy round the neck, and then, thrusting out his hip, he flung the other on to the hard floor, kneeling on him immediately and pressing the point of the hunting knife to his throat. Gwydion saw, with some grim satisfaction, that his mother had moved forward to shut the door, so that the struggle might not be witnessed by the homecoming war-band.

Then he had no time to notice anything else, for Math was struggling hard to throw him off, and was trying to set the horn to his lips, even though he lay prostrate. With a sharp kick, Gwydion drove the hand that held the horn away, and pressed down with such force that the breath was knocked from Math's body.

'Is there a cord, mother?' he gasped. 'If we could tie him, I need not silence him any other way.'

The woman began to tear strips from her linen gown, but before she could bring them to Gwydion, Math swung upwards with a great effort and opened his mouth to shout. Gwydion acted instantly, like a nervous animal, and struck the prince a blow on the temple with the coral haft of his knife. Math's head nodded and his eyes rolled back. He fell to the floor again and was silent.

Now the first of the victorious war-party began to file through the stockade gates. Gwydion looked at his mother anxiously. 'Mother,' he said, 'this has changed the situation. You could not stay here now, for Math is so crazed by fear of Caratacus, he would betray you. Now he has to avenge the blow I have given him. You must come with me.'

She gasped and said, 'Go, go, son, and leave me. I could not run. I should hold you back.'

Math was beginning to stir. Gwydion forced himself to strike him again, just hard enough to daze him once more. Then he grasped his mother's cloak and almost dragged her to the door. Once outside, he linked his arm in hers, smiled to a warrior who was staggering past the hut, his sword still dripping, and commented loudly how fine the night was for a walk round the stockade. Then, turning behind the hut into the shadow and away from the camp-fires, he pulled his mother towards the isolated prison-hut, just in time to see the dark shape of Gracchus clambering over the stakes. He called out softly to the Roman, who hesitated and then recognized him.

'Gracchus, my friend,' whispered Gwydion, 'Lean

down and help my mother over too. I will try to raise her from this side.'

It was something of a struggle, for Gracchus was exhausted from the long journey they had but recently made, and the sudden climb over the stockade had not been an easy exercise for such an elderly man as he was. Nevertheless, after some straining and panting, Gwydion's mother was sitting on the other side of the tall fence, begging them to go on and leave her. Then they heard the warning blasts of the horn, and knew that Math was beginning the hue-and-cry.

Gwydion almost dragged his mother to her feet and set her on the quietest of the horses; then he and Gaius mounted the other, leaving the third for the centurion, who was a heavily built man.

Even as they clapped heels to their horses' flanks, the torches flared inside the stockade, and Gwydion saw a stream of men running towards the gate nearest to where the horses had stood.

An arrow whistled through the air, falling short; then another, and another, this time well within range, and too close to be treated lightly. 'We must ride now, mother,' he said, 'or this will be the end of the journey for us all!' And then, leading the way through the darkness, he struck his pony so hard on the neck with the scabbard of his knife that the wiry little beast leapt forward with the shock and plunged straightway down the rough and winding path that led towards the river.

Gwydion turned once and saw that his mother rode next, and that Gracchus was in the rear. Gaius hung on to Gwydion's belt, gasping with the sudden exertion, but glad in his heart at last to be away from that place of cruelty, that home of treachery.

Then the sound of horses' hooves came to them from the darkness on the hillside above, and with no thought of sparing their mounts, the escaping riders rammed their heels hard into their straining flanks and scarcely dared to think of what lay before them now.

Then, less than a mile away, they saw the great river before them, and at the same time heard their pursuers closing in behind them. 'We shall never reach that river, my friend,' said Gaius. 'But at least we shall try!'

Gwydion said, 'Gaius, I have my father's knife now. I shall take one of them with me at least before this ride is done!'

Part Four

1 · The Cave on the Hill

Then, without warning, a flight of arrows buzzed through the darkness behind them, drawn at a venture by their pursuers. At first the boys thought that their party had escaped harm. Then their own pony shuddered beneath them, and stumbled, throwing them headlong on to the rocky path, and rolling over, a murderous shaft piercing his side. Neither boy was injured by the fall, yet now their situation was desperate for already they heard their followers approaching along the hard causeway.

'Mount my horse,' said the mother, reigning beside them; but the centurion would have none of this. He leaped to the ground and flung his reins towards Gwydion. 'Mount,' he said, 'and see your mother safely over the stream. Be assured, I shall not be long behind you.' Then he turned and disappeared into the night, running towards their pursuers.

There was nothing to be done. Gwydion wanted to join the brave Roman, but there was no time for heroics now. He hoisted Gaius into the saddle this time, and, taking his mother's bridle, ran between the two horses towards the river.

There they paused for a moment, on the rocky bank, then they forced their horses into the stream and made a courageous start at least to the crossing. At first the water swirled up about them, almost dragging Gwydion under, but he held tightly to the bridles, and encouraged the frightened horses to battle against the current.

The water was so icy cold that Gwydion's teeth chattered and after a while his limbs became numb; yet there was nothing to be done about such discomfort. The party had to keep going, using every ounce of strength against the sweep of the river.

Once Gwydion's fingers slipped from Gaius's bridle, and he almost fell, helpless, in the middle of the torrent, but Gaius leaned over and supported him, thrusting his arm beneath Gwydion's armpits and hanging on to him until the boy had found a new hold. And once Gwydion's mother, caught by a sudden onrush of the current, almost slipped from the saddle; but her sturdy Silurian pony bucked and curvetted in the water so gamely against the stream that she was flung back, and then clung tightly to the creature's neck, her reins now abandoned.

Thus, at length, dripping and chilled to the marrow, they found themselves wading through the rocky shallows at the far side of the river, the dread water crossed. When they had mounted the grass-grown bank above the stream, they halted, staring into the blackness from which they had just come. It seemed that there were shouts and cries from the other side, but in the darkness and with a strong night-wind blowing across to the east, it was impossible to be sure that the sounds they heard were those of men, and not of some prowling creatures of the night, such as frequented this misty area of marshland and woods.

Then, when they had given up hope and felt sure that they would never see the brave Roman again, Gaius, peering across the water, shouted, 'Someone is coming! Yes, a horseman; it is my father!'

In spite of his numbed limbs, he ran to the river bank as his father's horse stumbled out of the water on the slippery rocks. The centurion was shivering with cold, but he smiled as he came up to them. Gwydion saw that the front of his tunic was torn and smeared with blood. The centurion said, 'That was an unlucky slash from a long sword – but it has only broken the skin, my lad! Have no fear for me! Come on, they are afraid to ride into the river as yet, for it is one of their gods and they must pray to it for permission before they dare follow us. That will give us a little time.'

Gaius said, 'You have got yourself a fine horse, father! Did the owner give you his permission?'

The Romans laughed, and even Gwydion's mother joined in, amused at the boy's irony in such a desperate situation. The centurion said, 'Two of them over there will not need horses again. I took the strongest-looking beast, and I can tell you, he is a good swimmer! A real horse for a heavy man, such as I am!'

Gwydion said, 'How did you do it, Gracchus?'

The centurion laughed; 'An old trick,' he said. 'I waited for them and rolled a boulder down the path among the horses as they galloped in the darkness. The first one went down, and some of the others on top of him. They were galloping so fast that they could not stop. I do not think they even knew what had happened. Then I was amongst them, finding another steed for myself, and trying to put paid to an enemy or two. I can tell you, in a desperate fight, a handy boulder is as good as anything! Especially if you are struggling in the dark. A sword is so clumsy when you can't see what you are doing with it – but a good round stone can be used at close quarters, and you do not find it difficult to locate the target with such a weapon!'

Then he stiffened and listened. 'Come,' he said, 'we waste precious time. I think that their prayers are over now. I can hear them shouting for our blood!'

Once more the riders mounted and turned their horses' heads to the north. If they kept the river always to their left hand and the thick woodland to their right, they must, if the gods were kind to them, come at last to the territory of Madog of the Ordovices. But that was three days' riding before them – and not one of that band felt sure in his heart that they would ever see Madog and his friendly tribesmen. Now the going was a little better, for there was a road of sorts that ran in the direction they followed, though here and there it was broken by little tributary streams, or even by stretches of river marshland. All the same, their horses were now able to set a good pace, and after a while the sodden clothes that covered the backs of the fugitives did not seem quite so chilly, and the blood began to race in their veins again with the swift movement through the night.

Every few miles they stopped for a space, largely to let Gwydion's mother stretch her limbs, for she was unused to riding for any distance, though always she protested that they were treating her like a child, that they seemed to forget she was the widow of a warrior and the mother of a warrior-to-be, by the look of him! The centurion now knew her well enough to tease her a little, though he did this with all courtesy and respect, for he recognized in her those fine qualities of endurance which his people prized so highly and thought that they alone possessed.

Then, when their spirits were mounting and they had almost come to believe that their pursuers had abandoned the search, Gwydion put up his hand for silence, and through the mists, from a great distance, they heard distinctly the long wailing of a horn, the signal that their enemies were now on their track once more. The centurion said, 'We have a good start. Let us gallop on for another few miles, and then, if the opportunity occurs, let us turn off from the road. We may find a suitable place where we can hide. Then they can ride on to Ultima Thule for all we care!'

After half an hour, the woodland to their right thinned out a little and the land there became rocky again, and rose towards some gaunt hills. As they reached this spot, the centurion swung his horse in the direction of the rough slope, and they followed him, for now he was their leader. Once, as they were walking beside their horses when the going was difficult, the sound of the horn came to them again, and they even thought that the noise of hooves was wafted on the breeze to them. They must not delay now, they thought, and after a struggle, gained what seemed to be the summit of the first hill. While the centurion stayed with the party, Gwydion went round the peak of the hill to search for a resting-place. He came back after a short space and said that he had found a cave, away from the road, where they might shelter both themselves and the horses, for it was important that their beasts should not be observed from the road.

The centurion was delighted with the place. It would even be possible to light a fire there, he said, without being seen – if only they had flint and tinder. Now Gwydion's mother smiled at them.

'You warriors are very strong and brave,' she said, 'but you are not always thoughtful. Now a woman is always prepared for such occasions!' She opened the pouch which she wore at her belt and took out an ivory tinder-box, wrapped round with a length of doe skin. It had escaped the waters of the river, and after the boys had gathered a heap of bracken and branches, the centurion was able to strike the spark which set the fire alight.

The cave mouth was a narrow one, so low, in fact, that at first the horses were afraid to enter by it; though once they were inside, they seemed contented, and were soon grazing at the armful of grass which Gwydion brought in from the hillside lower down.

In a short while, the party were drying their wet clothes before the blaze and had regained something of their old spirits.

'If there were only anything to eat,' Gaius said, 'this would be almost an enjoyable experience.'

His father regarded him solemnly. 'When you grow up to become a legionary, you will have many nights such as these. I know, for I have endured them in Germany and Spain and even in Egypt. When you have a roof to your head, there is no food; and when there is food, you have to sleep out in a raging wind. A soldier never gets everything at one time – only bits and pieces, here and there, like scraps of meat flung to a dog!'

'Yet you love the soldier's trade, sir,' said Gwydion's mother, smiling.

'It is the only trade I know, madam,' said the centurion, becoming playfully formal, to echo the woman's tone. 'I have no doubt there are other trades almost as good, though I cannot conceive any profession being quite as worthwhile as that of a legionary in the Emperor's Legions.'

Then he fell silent, for far down below he heard the sound of horses' hooves and the shouting of a party of riders. He hung his cloak over the cave mouth, so that no shaft of light might strike across the rocks, to give warning of their presence. At last the sound of hooves fell away, and the party sat down again, about the fire, breathing more easily.

Later the boys went out and foraged for fuel. They brought back fir-cones and rushes, dry grass and dead wood – enough to last the night through. Then they all settled down to sleep, for, as the centurion said, since they were for the most part unarmed, there was little point in setting a watch. If they were found, it would be impossible to put up any lasting defence against such a superior number of pursuers. The logical thing was for them all to get a good night's sleep if the gods would allow it, so that they might be fresh to ride again when dawn broke.

But for Gwydion, whose head was confused by the many impressions of that strange day, there was little sleep. He lay near the mouth of the cave, staring out at the stars now, and wondering what the morrow might have in store for them all. Occasionally he rose and fed the fire, so that the cave would not become chilly. Once or twice he went to talk to one of the horses, which was restless and kept beating with one of its hooves on the floor of the cave. At length, Gwydion saw the dawn rise, its pale saffron fingers slowly feeling across the wooded hills to the east, lighting up the sleeping world with ghostly rays, at once hopeful and yet melancholy.

Gwydion stood outside the cave and looked across that great forest which covered the land, almost to the plains on the eastern sea-board. It was a great, dark island, he thought, full of magic and of cruelty. Only here and there, along the hill ridges, did men till the land and build their comfortable houses. So much of Britain was a wilderness, where wild beasts roamed, and where men almost as wild as the beasts held their festivals of blood and suffering. Britain was a land of many peoples, not one, he thought; many peoples who had come to the island at different times since the rising of the first sun, each conquering those who had got there before, each treating the others as slaves, as sacrifices, as less than men.

As the boy speculated on the land of his birth, he began to wonder why the Romans had even bothered to come to Britain. What he had seen of Roman Gaul was good; it was a well-regulated land, with good roads, inns, and houses; a land where men paid their taxes in money, not in blood – and where, in return for those taxes, they were given something of value, the protection of the greatest army the world had ever known. Gwydion was at heart a serious boy who had thought a great deal about these things since he had first seen the Roman army in action. Had his father lived, it is probable that he would never have had the opportunity of comparing the life of the tribes with that lived by the citizens of Rome; but now that he had travelled, there was a doubt in his mind – the doubt that, after all, the Belgic way might not be the true way of life.

He was about to rouse the centurion, who had asked to be wakened at dawn, to tell him about these thoughts, when something happening in the valley drove these ideas from his mind. He did indeed waken the centurion, but placed his hand over the man's mouth before he did so, and then he led him outside without saying a word. Together the two looked down in consternation.

Perhaps half a mile below them, a line of men were beating the bracken with their spear-shafts, fanned out round the hill, and approaching the summit with gradual steps.

The centurion pulled Gwydion down behind a boulder, lest one of the men, looking up from his task, should sight them. 'They must have been following our tracks in the soft road,' he said, 'and have come back here when the tracks finished. I had not thought of that, in the darkness.'

Gwydion said, 'These men are Silures, born hunters. They go as much on tracks as a dog on the nose. No doubt they have circled the hill, and are working up it from the road side too.'

The centurion said, 'If they are, they will soon be here, for there is little cover on that side for them to search. There is no time to lose now. Waken your mother and Gaius, and I will follow and lead out the horses.'

Gwydion did as he was bid, and then, with no thought of food or drink, no thought indeed of anything but escape, they mounted in the shelter of the boulders and began to ride down the hillside, towards the road, Gwydion and Gaius once more sharing a horse.

As their horses' hooves clattered on the stones, the beaters near the road looked up and saw them. Some ran for their horses, which were tethered a few hundred yards away, in a coppice, while the others stood their ground, on foot, raising their javelins threateningly.

The centurion set his horse's head at the point where the line was thinnest, and clapped his heels to the beast's sides. Then the party rode down, through the thin bracken, shouting, and so hoping to intimidate their enemies.

The boys saw the dark painted faces coming towards them, grinning horribly, and then a javelin flashed towards them, twisting in the first sunlight as it whistled through the air. They lowered their heads, and turned away from the weapon. The gods must have been on their side, for it swerved in the air, caught by the breeze that rushed down the hillside with the dawn, and missed them narrowly, burying itself deep in the flinty soil behind them.

Gwydion looked back to see a feathered warrior run

at his mother and take her bridle strongly in both hands, dragging down on the struggling horse to bring her to a stop. Then the centurion was on him, reigning back his big horse so that it towered above the dark head of the tribesman. Gwydion turned away as the heavy hooves came down and the man shrieked and tumbled in the bracken, writhing.

Then they were through the line and out on to the road again. Yet behind them came the sound of pursuing hooves once more, and now the boys knew that their enemies would have no mercy.

Now all but Gwydion had slept well that night, and they were fresh, as their horses were; while their attackers had spent much of the night seeking them, and already flagged a little.

Then Gwydion saw his mother do a strange thing; she suddenly stood in her stirrups, for she rode in the manner of Belgic women, and tore off her cloak, flinging it behind her into the road. Then she flung away her heavy sheepskin jacket, so as to ride lightly.

Gwydion smiled at this, even though death rode at their heels, for it meant that his mother was casting off the caution of her long domestic years, and remembering that once she, too, had ridden to the hunt, like all Celtic girls, and had even taken on the boys in mock jousts with ash staves. He called back, 'Hail, Mother of Warriors!' but his mother only made a wry face at him, and then galloped on.

2 · 'Consider Yourselves Under Arrest!'

By the time the sun was rising in the heavens, they had shaken off the greater number of their pursuers; though three Silures rode well ahead of their fellows, each one being anxious, it seemed, to take the first prisoner. The centurion shouted back to them once that he would give battle to any two of them if they would let his friends go free, but they only laughed at him, and one of them swung a sling in the air, from the saddle, his missile narrowly missing the Roman. Then the centurion rode alongside the boys and shouted that he had a mind to stay back and grapple with two of them, and hope to throw them to the ground, so impeding the attack for a while. But Gaius swore that if his father did this, he too would stay behind, for it was his turn to try what combat felt like. His father told him that he was an obstinate Roman wolf-cub, blood-brother to Romulus and Remus, and that when he got him home he would thrash him for disobeying his father. Then, with a grim smile, the centurion fell back to protect the rear of the party and the chase continued.

Soon they came to a stretch of the road where the woodland encroached on the man-made highway, as though Nature were taking her revenge on man's impertinence. As they broke through the screen of trees and bushes, they saw before them, to the right, a dried-up stream-bed, which seemed to lead between the hills, and to become a gully. Almost without thought, Gwydion reined his horse into the cleft, to be followed im-

mediately by his mother and the centurion. The Roman
was shouting, 'That was a mistake, my friend, but we
must keep together now!'

And indeed, as they went further, Gwydion saw how
right the older man had been, for now on either side
the walls of the gully closed them in. If an enemy could
keep abreast of them, on the higher level, he would
find it relatively easy to pick them off with arrows since
their opportunities for evasive action below were so re-
stricted.

Ahead of them, and to the left again, stretched the
hillside, covered with woodland. If they could reach
that spot, then they might yet find a more suitable bolt-
hole; but as yet it was the best part of a mile away, and
already they heard their enemies approaching behind
them.

Then a shout from above them caused them to look
up, and they saw what they had feared; the Silurians,
spaced out now as they outdid each other in the chase,
silhouetted against the morning sky, already drawing
their bows as they rode, their reins flying loose.

The first flight of arrows rattled on the cliff wall beside them; but of the next swarm, one shaft struck Gaius in the shoulder, so that he reeled behind Gwydion and had to grip tight round his friend's waist to keep himself from falling, with the shock of pain. The centurion, seeing what had happened, rode alongside and broke off the shaft, which projected on both sides of the lad's shoulder. So he drew out the barb, and then rode beside Gwydion, supporting the swaying body of his son.

As he did this, there was a shout from the pursuers above, for they were warriors themselves and respected courage in others. They did not use their bows again, but contented themselves with sending stones from their slings from time to time, in an attempt to wound not the riders, but their horses.

Now, it seemed, their enemies were confident. Glancing back, Gwydion saw that the other half of the attacking force was riding behind them up the dry gully, so cutting off their chance of doubling on their tracks and making their way out to the road again. It seemed that this was the end of the journey, when suddenly the cen-

turion said, 'Look ahead, there is a tongue of rock that
enters the gully. If we can swerve on to it, we can re-
mount the hillside on the opposite side from them, keeping the river-bed between us. Then we might gain the
woods!'

He called back this plan to Gwydion's mother, whose
face was now drawn and tired, and who rode her mount
as though she might fall at any moment from sheer exhaustion.

At last the narrow step of rock came towards them,
and almost without reining in, Gwydion turned on to
it. His horse stumbled for a moment, under its heavy
load, and then regained its footing and was breasting
the rocky slope. The centurion stayed to the last, and
then, amid a hail of angry sling-shots from the disappointed Silures, he joined them in the struggle up the
slope.

But the tired, wounded party never entered that inviting wood; nor did they wish to when they had reached
higher levels of the hill, for they found that a narrow
road ran along its summit, and as they gasped for their
breath and almost came near to moaning from the cruel
exertion of their ride, a party of men appeared on that
road, marching out from beyond the shadow of the trees
in perfect order, singing a rough soldiers' lilt as they
went, their pikes set jauntily across their armoured
shoulders, their round Roman helmets dangling from
the shafts of their pikes, their water-bottles rattling on
their long shields, which were slung from their backs.
Gracchus looked at them with a strange expression of
ecstasy, then leaping from his weary horse, he began to

run towards them, singing and shouting all in one breath, calling them brothers and giving his official titles and rank.

The singing of the company of legionaries stopped abruptly. A grey-haired officer who rode at the rear of the men trotted up on his lithe Barbary horse, shouting an order. A dozen pikemen rushed forward, unslinging helmet and javelin as they went. Gwydion, looking down the hill, saw the Silurians halt and draw back, then he felt Gaius' hands relax, and turned in time to prevent the boy from falling in a faint to the rocks. At the same moment, their pony, who had borne them both bravely over many cruel miles, gave a deep sigh and sank to his knees beneath them. The two boys rolled slowly among the stones, Gwydion doing his best to keep his friend's wounded shoulder from striking on the sharp flints.

When he rose, the Silurians were in flight, bending round as they galloped, to shoot their last defiant but futile arrows towards the Romans on the hill. Gracchus was talking to the commander, who was shaking his head gravely, as though in some doubt. Gwydion's mother had dismounted from her horse and was bending stiffly over Gaius, to whose cheeks a little colour was at last returning.

The centurion said to the officer, 'But I assure you, sir, that is the situation. It will be confirmed from my record, which has always been a good one. I beg you to believe me. I speak on the honour of a centurion, a true Roman, who has never once even thought of betraying his country.'

The officer nodded, dispassionately. 'That will be decided,' he said, 'when we reach headquarters. In the meantime, you are all to consider yourselves under arrest.'

Gwydion said to a legionary who was hanging his helmet back on his javelin, 'Where is headquarters, Roman?'

The man scratched his cropped black head. 'Up there,' he said, jerking back his calloused thumb. 'I can't rightly recall the name. It's one of those barbarian names, you know. But one place is the same as any other place to a soldier, lad! You'll be all right there, have no fear; the commandant has been in Britain so long, why, he looks like a Briton!'

Then with soldiers on either side of them, Gracchus and Gwydion began to march back towards Vricon. His mother and Gaius were allowed a place in the baggage-wagon, where the wounded boy fell into a troubled sleep, for by now his wound was becoming inflamed, though the company surgeon, who also rode in the wagon, assured them that it was not a poisoned wound.

'And that is something to thank the gods for,' he said. 'It is not often that a Silurian shoots an arrow unless he has made sure first! They are not pleasant fighters. They use too much of that foxglove juice on their edged weapons for my liking. I'd rather deal with a straight slash any day than a mere prick that has been doctored by those black-faced cannibals!'

In the end, Gwydion's mother told the doctor to be quiet as he was rattling on too much and disturbing the boy. The doctor was very hurt for a time, but at last swallowed his pride and said that if he had such a woman as a nurse at his headquarters hospital, he would get promotion to Major before the year was out.

'Perhaps,' said Gwydion's mother, 'You'd also get used to working with a gag in your mouth, my man!'

After which the surgeon hardly spoke a word until they came in sight of the camp-fires, late that evening.

3 · Roman Justice!

That night Gwydion and his mother sat on a hard wooden bench, aching in every limb from their journey, in the anteroom of the Roman commandant. Gaius was sleeping peacefully now in their own tent, tended by a young doctor who had been taken by the boy's bravery when the wound was burned to drive out the fever in it. 'He will heal perfectly,' he said. 'Within a week, why, this game young hawk will hardly know that he was ever nicked by a tribesman's arrow. Rest assured, madam, this one will live to fight for Rome; have no fear.'

So she and Gwydion were taken under escort to wait in the bare anteroom, until the commandant called them in for questioning. Gracchus had been marched in under strong guard, and they had even taken the precaution of manacling his wrists, since he was apparently a strong man, and one who might break out and do the commandant an injury under questioning.

Now they waited, wondering what was about to happen; wondering whether life had indeed been as kind as they had thought, when it allowed them to stumble into that squad of legionaries on top of the rocky hill.

Gwydion said to his mother, 'What will happen to us, mother?'

She shrugged her shoulders and said, 'If they think we are spies they may execute us. If they think we are merely stray followers of Caratacus, they will make us slaves. If they believe us and come to accept our word that we are true Belgae, well, who knows, they may even set us free – to wander back to our own territory and starve there!'

Gwydion looked up at his mother to see whether she was joking, but her face was set, and he knew then that she meant every word she had said.

He was silent for a while; then he began to question her again, but she cut him short. 'Gwydion, son,' she said. 'What happens to us is hardly important. We are a defeated race, and we must understand that. But what happens to good Gracchus is another matter. He is a faithful soldier of the Empire, and should they accuse him of being a deserter, as it seems they intend to do, then they would be killing an innocent man.'

Gwydion said, 'But, mother, we could prove that he was a good, true man. Surely they would listen to my testimony.'

The rough, good-natured legionary who stood near the commandant's door, on guard, heard this, and smiled at the boy. 'Rome is liable to do many strange things, my friend,' he said, 'but that would be the strangest!'

Gwydion was angry at the man's tone, and almost rose to speak his mind to him; but just then the soldier placed his gnarled finger to his lips, and stood smartly to attention. The door opened and Gracchus walked out, smiling, his wrists free of manacles. Gwydion began to run towards him, then stopped in surprise. A Roman officer was following the centurion; an officer with thin, fair hair and very tired eyes; the officer to whom he had been taken that night after Camulodunum! The commandant! Gwydion looked at him with an uncertain smile, and the Roman came forward and put his hand on the boy's shoulder.

'Well, Gwydion,' he said, 'thank you for looking after this silly old soldier of mine! Without you, Rome would have lost a good pensioner!'

Gwydion said, 'Not a pensioner, sir – a centurion!'

But the commandant wiped his hand across his forehead, as though he was very tired, and had read too many reports that day. He said, 'No, there you are wrong, for once, my friend! Allow me to know better this time! Gracchus has served Rome well, and was almost at the end of his service. Now, in view of the information which he brings back about the disposition of the forces in Siluria, I have been able to discharge him honourably, and even to increase his pension! That is so, isn't it, Gracchus?'

The centurion turned, his face serious. 'Yes, it is, sir,' he said. 'But that's your idea, not mine. No one shall ever say that I begged my release. I am prepared to go on serving Rome till my time has been served, aye, and even longer than that, if there is a place for me in the Legion.'

The officer patted him gently on the shoulder. 'Get on with you, you old fire-eater,' he said. 'Won't you ever grow up! Why, I should be only too glad if the Emperor said to me what I have just said to you! But, alas, he won't! A hard, hard man, that Emperor of ours, Gracchus.'

Then his tone changed. He came forward and said, 'Gwydion, introduce me to your mother, about whom I've heard such glowing words from Gracchus here.'

Gwydion said, 'But aren't you going to question us, sir?'

The officer said, 'There's only one question I want to ask. It is this: how are you going to like having Gracchus for your god-father?' He stood back and smiled at the look on the lad's face. Then Gwydion's mother put her arm round the boy's shoulders as she smiled at the officer. 'Did that old ruffian of a centurion say that he was going to look after me?' she said.

The officer said, 'That is the main reason for my giving him his discharge from the Legion, madam. We recognize our duties to Britain, you know, in spite of all the harsh things you Celts think of us!'

Now Gracchus was swaying from foot to foot, his weathered face wrinkled in a self-conscious smile. He was too shy to speak.

'Well,' said Gwydion's mother at last, 'I must say that you breed fine soldiers in Rome, sir; warriors who cannot even ask their own questions, but must hop about from one foot to the other like country youths trying to ask a maiden to ride with them to the May Fairing!'

The officer smiled. 'Oh, he would have asked you himself, Madam, if we had given him time, no doubt! but time is pressing and I don't want him to wait another six months before he can screw up his great courage to talk to you! You see, we have a good ship leaving the Abus for Southern Gaul in a week or so and, if your agreement had been arranged by that time, you would then be legally entitled to travel with him to his place of retirement, since he has volunteered to take responsibility for the upbringing of your son.'

His mother was now looking so cross that Gwydion almost became afraid. But he walked over to the centurion and took his hand. 'Don't worry,' he said, 'I am not going to let this chance slip even if mother is! I proclaim you my god-father before the commandant. That makes it legal, doesn't it?'

Then Gwydion's mother had to laugh, and so, walking beside the centurion she led the way to the tent-door, saying she was anxious to visit Gaius and to see how his wound was progressing. Then suddenly she turned as though a thought had struck her.

'My folk farm among the Atrebates in Gaul,' she said. 'How would it suit you, centurion, to share our home and settle down there!'

Gracchus smiled, but gravely, for this was a new development in the situation, and one which had to be treated with care, in view of the sensitivity with which most Celts regarded the question of hospitality.

'That sounds well,' he said. 'But before we settle on

anything, I would like you to inspect that little place I have in Lugdunum. That is, if the commandant can arrange for Rome to turn it back to me!'

But this time the commandant seemed to be in no mood to appreciate jests. He looked up from his maps and orders of the day, his thin smile frozen on his weary face. He surveyed Gracchus tiredly for a moment, as was his habit when confronted by senior non-commissioned officers who overstepped the mark, but could not be punished like ordinary legionaries. Then he looked away, seeming to find an interest in a tall wine-flask that stood, empty and forlorn in a corner of the tent, the receptacle only of flowers that some thoughtful slave had brought in from the woods above the camp that morning to please the great one. It was a very ordinary flask, not at all beautiful. In fact, they were thrown overboard by dozens when Roman ships docked at any of the ports along the eastern shore – often because they formed part of a cargo that the military had contracted to carry to Britain, but which had somehow become depleted on the way across. An ordinary flask. Yet he seemed to like looking at it. Then, when Gracchus was already beginning to feel like a very small boy, beginning to feel the confidence oozing out of his palms and his boot-soles, the commanding officer spoke. His voice was now cold and official.

'That will be a matter of form, centurion,' he said. 'You must not bother me with trifles. It is your right, and consequently Rome will respect it.'

Gracchus saluted. 'I should not have said that, I know, sir,' he said, 'but sometimes, as one knocks about the world, one meets so much duplicity, so much double-dealing, that one becomes over-cautious.'

The officer raised a tired head from his documents and allowed his lips to smile at the soldier, but it was not a smile that most men would be glad to see.

'Yes, my friend,' he said, 'but we are speaking of Rome now; and when it comes to Rome, one is always sure. Don't you agree, centurion?'

Gracchus clicked his heels together as smartly as he could on the grass of the tent-floor.

'Of course, sir,' he said. 'Of course!'

But all the same, he was glad to have the officer's word for it; and glad, too, to be outside that tent again, for Gracchus was a soldier through and through, and like all other soldiers he knew that though military law was a fine thing, a splendid thing, a most glorious thing, it could also turn out to be a very dangerous thing – especially when dispensed by tired, and rather overworked officers!

Outside the tent, Gwydion's mother smiled at him, and he knew just what she was thinking. He did not dare to meet her eyes for a moment. Then suddenly, as though forcing herself to a decision which must be spoken quickly if it were to be spoken at all, she said, 'Our gods are different, friend; our way of life is different, and I, like you, am too old now to learn new ways. But it runs in my mind that I have seen the best of the old dispensation and that it will never be so good again among my people. I would want my son to know an ordered world, where men know the law and obey it and where blood is not spilled in waste. I cannot come with you to Lugdunum, Gracchus, but I would want you to take my son. Take Gwydion and teach him your ways. Make him into a Roman, if you choose, but one like yourself, centurion. Then I shall be proud of him, as I am certain his father would have been proud of him. Yes, you will make him a fine man, centurion, albeit a Roman!'

Gracchus mumbled in embarrassment and even put out his big spear-calloused hand to touch her arm in sympathy; but already, overcome by her own feelings, she had moved swiftly among the tents and was gone.

Gracchus stared after her. 'Yes, you shall live to be proud of him, madam,' he said almost vehemently, 'or may men spit on me in the streets as I pass. But I'll never make him fight for Rome, I promise you, unless he chooses to of his own free will!'

Then, as though suddenly ashamed of talking to himself in this manner in the darkness, he turned smartly, as a soldier should, and marched back to his billet.

4 · Math Comes Again

Only one other occasion of note happened before the party boarded the wagon that would take them across Britain to the Abus. The night before they left, Gwydion was playing dice with Gaius in the tent of the young doctor, when a guard came to the tent-flap and said, 'Master Gwydion, there's a visitor to see you.'

Gwydion said, 'A visitor? Who can that be? Where is he?'

The soldier said, 'He is outside the palisade, we couldn't let him in without permission. He's a black-haired fellow, of about your own age. Wears feathers in his helmet, he does, and coloured trews. I should say he's a chieftain of sorts among the southern folk. He wouldn't give his name. He just ordered me to fetch you out to him. Cheek, I call it!'

Gaius said, 'That is Math. He wishes to make friends again, Gwydion.'

Gwydion considered for a moment and then said, 'What if he wishes to trap me; to entice me outside and then take his revenge for the indignity I have done him? One sudden thrust in the dark, and he would have his revenge.'

Gaius said, 'Get the soldier to arrest him, then we shall know.'

But Gwydion only said, 'No, let him go free, back to his own folk. The day when I wanted his friendship is past.'

The soldier nodded and went out, to send Math away from the Roman camp, and Gwydion and Gaius went on with their game again. Now they had their own life before them, a new life and a fine life. They were contented with what fate had brought them. Nor did they once spare a thought for Math. They did not see the look which passed over his face when the guard ordered him roughly to be gone. They did not see the dejection which his sagging body spoke as he climbed slowly into his saddle. Nor did they see the direction in which he rode, his head bent forward on his chest, his hands hanging loosely at his sides, as his horse took which way it willed, finally setting its head towards those dark woods which covered the sullen face of the land.

Epilogue - AD 51

The Bridge at Lugdunum

In the long slanting rays of the late afternoon sun, two young men stood on the bridge at Lugdunum, lounging on the stone parapet and looking at each other, and laughing again and again, as though their lives had suddenly become very happy. One was a tall, fair-haired man with blue eyes, dressed in the fashion of a prosperous farmer of the area, his long hair plaited and braided, a well-worn but sound leathern tunic about his upper body, a bronze-studded belt about his waist, his long legs covered by dark green frieze trews, cross-gartered with strips of yellow hide. On his feet were strong caligulae, thick-soled and bound with heavy nails, to which the red-brown soil still clung. His companion was shorter, but broader in the shoulder, dark-haired and deeply tanned by the weather. This man was dressed in the uniform of a decurion of the Legions, his breastplate well-burnished, the knot of coloured ribbons at his shoulder, just above the loricae, fluttering in the early evening breeze. His long dress-boots were laced along the shin with silver wires, and were well polished in contrast to those of his friend. He held his round steel helmet under his left arm, and often gestured with his other hand, to emphasize a point he was making. He seemed confident and definite in everything he said; while his companion was a little more serious, perhaps more hesitant, and perhaps more deep-thinking.

They turned for a moment and looked over the balustrade of the bridge, down towards the broad stream. The Roman pointed down to the river bank and the other followed his gaze. Then they both began to laugh again.

'You gave them more than they expected that day, brother,' said Gaius, smiling at his fair-haired companion. Gwydion nodded and pursed his lips as though remembering a time long past. The Roman dug him in the ribs playfully and said, 'And you could give most of us a good fight now, by the feel of the muscle in your back! Farming seems to suit you, otherwise I'd try to persuade you to join me in the Legion again! But I know that would be hopeless!'

Gwydion said, 'I have had enough of fighting just for the sake of it! My folk were always farmers at heart, and I am happy now, looking after father's acres and herds. Besides, the old man needs someone to keep an eye on him while you are away. He's still just a boy at heart!'

Gaius laughed again. 'He could still give us more than we bargained for, if we forgot our manners! He will never forget that he was a centurion once, and that I am only a decurion. Sometimes he speaks to me as though he were still in camp, giving out his orders for the next day's routine!'

Gwydion said, 'Well, my mother's just the same! She can never forget that she ran the farm at Camulodunum! I get up to Northern Gaul about three times a year, when the wagons run, and present a report of my doings to her. And woe betide me if I seem a little late with the milking, or if I haven't got the corn-seed in at the right time! She still looks after the dairy up there, and if anyone as much as puts his nose round the door, she skelps him out with a wooden ladle! Yes, they run all right! There's no nonsense about it when she makes an attack! "If I can handle a centurion," she says, "a real Roman centurion, none of your native officers, I can handle you!" And believe me, Gaius, I've seen warriors run when she goes for them! Men who would stand up without body-armour and face a chariot sweep!'

They laughed again, and then Gaius said, 'Shall we borrow a boat from someone and row down the river while the sun still lasts?'

Gwydion said, 'No, it is better here. We have much to say to each other before they send you back to Britain, and we can talk better on the bridge than in a boat.'

The other smiled and said, 'Perhaps you are right. If we were ever in a boat again, I should remember that old tub which carried us from Armorica to Vectis, and I should feel sorry about that poor Roman officer, who was only doing his duty when they sank him with the boulder.'

Gwydion said, 'I wonder whether Gryf ever got that paper? I sent a wagon-man with it, but never heard whether he got it in the end.'

The Roman said, 'I don't suppose he worries, really. He is probably too occupied with that young son of his, teaching him how to be a pirate, like his father! Gryf was a rogue, and no mistake, but the sort of rogue who will make a good citizen one day! Rome needs a few rogues in it to counteract the stupid statesmen who always seem to undo the good work that the soldiers do!'

A dark cloud seemed to settle for a moment over Gwydion's red face. 'I hope that the statesmen don't undo the good work which you and your men have just finished, anyway,' he said gravely.

Gaius said, 'You mean Caratacus?'

The other nodded. 'Yes,' he said. 'Now that Rome has finally broken that man's pride and we have him prisoner and in Gaul, let us hope that the Emperor Claudius will treat him as he deserves, for all the suffering he has caused. Let us hope that Caratacus is never allowed to raise the tribes again, disturbing men's lives and putting innocent ones to the sword. How can men work and till the land and harvest their crops if such madmen as Caratacus are allowed to carry on their ambitious ways unchecked?'

Gaius took his step-brother by the shoulders and looked into his face humourously. 'Why, old Gwydion,' he said, 'you are quite the solid Roman farmer these days! You *have* altered in five years, while I've been away in Britain. I never thought to hear you say things like that!'

Gwydion said, 'Well, you may laugh, brother, but in the fields, under the blue skies of Heaven, I have had many opportunities of thinking about life. And I have come to the conclusion that life isn't given to us just so that we can exert our strength on other men and turn their lives inside-out for our own advantage. . . . It takes us a long time to see sense, doesn't it, Gaius?'

The Roman nodded, a little sadly it seemed, as though he were being forced to admit to a thought which he had always held back from uttering. He said haltingly, 'Men have to travel many miles, and suffer many pains, before they see reason, very often. You have had to become a farmer, and I a soldier, to see it. But the only thing that matters is that . . . we have learned our lessons. Now we are a true family and a happy one; and one day, when I have finished my service, I shall come back here and shall join you on this good red earth, and help you to cut the corn and raise the beasts!'

Gwydion said, 'I'm not so sure about that! You'll be more handy with a javelin than a scythe! You can't cut corn with a short sword, you know, friend! You can't milk cows with your helmet on! The beast wouldn't take kindly to that!'

Gaius replied, 'Don't sneer at me, young brother! You'd look well marching with the Legion in your smock, with your milk-pail in your hand! Yes, come to think of it, I'd love to have you on the parade ground, presenting arms with your shepherd's crook!'

Gwydion pretended to be cross, and although he knew that it was against the law for any civilian to molest a Roman soldier, he took Gaius' arm suddenly and began to twist it behind his back, playfully. Gaius dropped his helmet, and swung round to take hold of his step-brother. 'All right, young Gwydion,' he said, laughing, 'I'll do what I didn't do before – I'll give you a ducking myself, this time!'

But even as he grasped the Celt about the waist, there was a sudden clattering of horses' hooves, and a party of auxiliaries cantered from a side road into the principal avenue.

Gaius stopped wrestling immediately and stooped towards his helmet. He put it on straight and stood erect on the pavement, so that no Roman soldier, barbarian or not, should see him behaving in a manner unfitting for an officer. Gwydion saw the expression of gravity come over his face, and gave a small giggle, which almost made Gaius burst out laughing again.

Then the auxiliaries drew nearer. 'These are new ones, from Britain, I think,' whispered Gaius, staring at them coldly as befitted a decurion with five years' service behind him, who expected a salute from this band of rough cavalry.

Then Gwydion drew in his breath with surprise. The leader of the party, a tall, eagle-faced man, wearing a bunch of heron feathers at the point of his leathern helmet, carried a little dog before him on the saddle, half-wrapped in the long regulation Roman blue riding-cloak.

'Why,' said Gwydion, 'that is a little dog almost the image of Bel, my Bel, the one I lost so long ago.'

The band of horsemen were now almost level with the two on the bridge. The leader called out harshly in Celtic and the riders half-turned and raised their right hands, palm upwards, towards the unsmiling decurion, who gravely returned their salute. Gwydion stared at their young leader, whose dark eyes pierced him through and through. He noted the long face, the swarthy skin, the thin and faintly smiling mouth, the long black hair knotted below the helmet.

The resemblance to Math was extraordinary, but it was not he. This man had a fine arrogance which Math lacked, even at the height of his power.

Suddenly the leader stopped and called his men to a halt with an imperious wave of the hand. They stood still in the avenue while their leader rode forward towards the balustrade of the bridge. He looked down at Gaius, his dark eyes mocking, but his mouth unsmiling. 'Have I your permission to speak with this civilian, decurion?' he asked, his dark and jewelled hand caressing the head of the little dog that lay across his broad sheepskin saddle.

Gaius said, 'I have no objection, trooper, if the citizen wishes to speak with you, that is.'

The horseman half-bowed with mock-gravity and respect. Then he leaped lightly from the saddle and put the small dog into Gwydion's hands.

'I journey far, my friend,' he said, 'on Rome's business; but not so fast that I do not recognize a fellow-countryman and, what is more, a man who loves a dog even as I do.'

He made a stiff military bow. 'Take the dog, comrade,' he said, 'and keep him well, as your own, for where I go there will be little time to think of dogs.'

Gwydion held the dog, looking down into its dark brown eyes and recalling Bel as he used to be, leaping and running in the woods, barking in the sunlight for the joy of being alive, of being with his master. He looked back at the young horseman, feeling the tears already gathering in his own eyes. 'Friend,' he said, 'ride on your way to what glory you shall find, and ride with a quiet mind for this is the sort of dog I have dreamed about. It is an omen to me.'

Then, on a sudden impulse, Gwydion handed the dog to Gaius, for he wished to embrace this Briton who had been so generous. Although the decurion was a little nonplussed at being forced to act the nursemaid before this troop of smiling foreign horsemen, who enjoyed seeing a stern-faced officer behaving like a human being for once, he was won over immediately when the dog began to lick his face, for, though he would never have admitted it, he had felt a little out of things when the two Celts got together so easily. Now the little dog was restoring the balance and showing that a Roman was as good a master as anyone else!

Just then the Celtic cavalryman turned, and seeing the Roman petting the dog said, 'It is good to know that one has a friend in this uncertain world – especially when that friend is one so eminent as a decurion!'

Gaius sensed the irony of the man's remark. He began to frown a little, just to show the man that he could not expect preferential treatment. Then his good-humour returned and he said, 'Don't be too sure of that, trooper. If you are ever late for parade while you are stationed in Lugdunum, I shall make it my special business to see that you get extra punishment! Moreover, I shall see that your rations are forthwith reduced and your pay stopped completely!'

The young Celt threw back his head and laughed at this, with an equal, good-tempered sarcasm. 'That would at least be a recognition on the part of Rome that I was entitled to rations and pay! And to tell the truth, decurion, I've hardly seen either since I took service under the Eagles!'

Gaius said, 'Perhaps the paymaster doesn't think you should have any until he is sure that you are worth it! We Romans have to be very careful with you savages, my friend!'

The horseman grinned and said, 'Well, I don't blame you! But we shall live down our bad record, and one day, mark my words, we shall send Britons to sit in the Senate in Rome, like any other citizens!' He bent his head closer to Gaius and said almost confidentially, 'And, a jest for a jest, there could come a time when your Emperor himself might be chosen from my own people! Such things are not unknown!'

Gaius smiled grimly and retorted, 'You try putting yourself up for election, my lad, and see what you'll get! Ten years confined to barracks, if I have my way!'

The horsemen had gradually clustered round the group on the bridge now, and laughed to hear the Roman officer teasing their proud young leader. But Gaius turned towards them and immediately their faces froze and their lips lost their smiles. They pulled their horses out on to the broad road again and sat motionless, like statues.

Gaius smiled. 'You have a well-drilled troop of horse here, my friend,' he said.

The young Celt shrugged his shoulders. 'Decurion,' he said a little wearily, 'I have had a troop of my own since I stood as high as your belt, and I dare say that what I don't know about controlling cavalry isn't in your Roman hand book!' He grinned at Gaius as he spoke, but the Roman, who usually discounted Gallic bravado, was prepared to take his words seriously.

'I think you are right, too,' he admitted. 'You are probably wasted with this band of cut-throats! You must cultivate a little ambition, young man, and aspire to become a sergeant of horse, one day. Say the word, and though it runs against my conscience, I will speak up for you to the captain tomorrow. You would look well at the head of a whole company.'

But the Celt only grinned and waved the suggestion aside. 'Sir,' he said softly, 'I who was once a lord in Britain could not hope to become a real Roman sergeant! No, I know my place, decurion!'

Gaius flushed at this, for it seemed to him that Rome was being made the jest of these barbarians. Gwydion too sensed the change in his friend's heart. He turned swiftly to the Celt and said, 'Yes, and your place is not here, on the bridge, with the cruel night wind coming up the river. Your place is at my father's table, drinking a cup of mead and sampling our ham and fresh bread. Can you not send your horsemen on to barracks and come back with us to supper. We are starved of news from Britain. Can he, decurion?'

Gaius said, 'It is against the rules.' The soldier nodded, as though he knew that this would be the inevitable answer.

'But,' went on Gaius with a sly smile, 'if I were to march them in, that would be in order.'

The horseman grinned cheekily. 'I should enjoy it

more if you rode at their head, sir,' he said. 'You would make a fine sight, heading this column of men, most of whom have hardly walked a step in their lives!'

But Gaius gave as good as he got. 'Don't worry, my friend,' he said. 'It is they who would make the fine sight, for I should dismount them and march them in, as I said! They shall learn a little Roman discipline whenever I take them in charge.'

For the first time the Celt's eyes widened in genuine concern. 'But, sir,' he said, 'that is something that not even Rome can do – make a British cavalryman march! It is unheard of! They would mutiny rather than that!'

Gaius pretended to consider for a while. 'Perhaps you are right, trooper,' he said. 'We can't have the British auxiliaries upset on their first night in Lugdunum, can we! Very well, they shall ride, and we'll all go with them! Then when I have spoken to your officer, we shall go back to the farm and celebrate our new friendship. Will that do, do you think?'

But without waiting for an answer, he turned towards the troop of horsemen, who were beginning to smile again, and putting on his parade-ground voice, bawled, 'Why, you undisciplined welter of unprincipled cut-throats, who do you think you are, simpering your stupid heads off in Lugdunum? Have you no respect for Rome? Have you no respect for the Emperor's uniform? Do you want me to flog the lot of you before lights-out? Do you, then? Who will give me an answer, eh?'

But they had seen the look on their own lord's face

and now they sat on their sheepskin saddles, almost lolling back, their long legs dangling at their horses' sides. They saw that their lord was already arm-in-arm with the fair-haired farmer who spoke Celtic, and they were unperturbed. They knew that this decurion was only trying to scare them! But they were men who had seen Romans before, many times, and in bloody battle. They knew that this one was their friend, despite his blustering voice. They grinned back at him and began to cheer.

There was nothing for it. Gaius had to laugh too. 'Come on,' he said, 'or this lot will get me into trouble!' Then he gave the order and they all began to move across the bridge. And as they went the little dog frisked round the heels of the stern-faced soldier, and the last rays of the Gallic sun fell across the broad river, turning its blue currents to a rich red gold. Tomorrow, it seemed, would be a good day.

Appendices

Place Names in the Story

Abus	The River Humber.
Armorica	Brittany.
Belgica	The Low Countries, the Netherlands.
Camulodunum	Colchester, the capital of the Belgae.
Carnac	In Brittany, famous for its stone circle.
Gaul	France.
Gesoriacum	Boulogne.
Londinium	London.
Lugdunum	Lyons.
Mai Dun	Maiden Castle.
Middle Sea	The Mediterranean.
Scythia	The area roughly north of the Black Sea.
Siluria	South Wales.
Sorbiodunum	Old Sarum.
Vectis	The Isle of Wight.
Vricon	Wroxeter, in Shropshire.

Locations of the Tribes Mentioned

Atrebates	The Arras area of France and Wiltshire and Berkshire in England.
Belgae	The Low Countries. In England, what is now Hertfordshire and Essex, with many allied and subject peoples south of the Thames. Their dominion stretched over the greater part of the South-East. These peoples, of mixed Celtic and Germanic stock, were the latest arrivals to Britain before the first Roman visit, under Julius Caesar. The Belgae probably came to Britain about the year 75 B.C.
Brigantes	The Dales folk of the Pennines; inhabitants of North-East Britain.
Cantii	Kent.
Durotriges	Dorset.
Iceni	Norfolk and Suffolk. This tribe revolted later under Boadicea.
Ordovices	North Wales.

Picts	A tribe of Caledonians, living in the North of Britain. Their name probably means 'The painted ones'.
Trinobantes	Essex. A subject people of the Belgae.
Veneti	A sea-going people of North-West Gaul.

Other Names and Words Mentioned in the Story

Aulus Plautius	The Roman General who commanded all the forces that invaded Britain in A.D. 43.
Caradoc	The Welsh manner of saying Caratacus, which is the Roman form of the name.
Cartismandua	The Queen of the Brigantes, who betrayed Caratacus to the Romans in the end.
Cunobelinus	The father of Caratacus; a great king of the Belgae. Shakespeare calls him 'Cymbeline'.
Romulus and Remus	The founders of Rome, said to have been suckled by a she-wolf.

THE ROMAN ARMY

Alae	A Latin word meaning 'wings'. These were Auxiliary cavalry troops who fought on the wings, or flanks, of a Legion, to protect the infantrymen.
Auxiliary	Roman soldiers recruited from subject peoples. They formed 'alae' and helped the Legionaries, who were Roman citizens by birth.
Centurion	A Roman commander of a hundred men.
Decurion	A commander of ten men.
The Eagles	The Legions; so-called from the eagle which surmounted the Roman standard.
Legion	About 5,000 infantry and 120 riders for messages and scouting.

GENERAL

Caligulae	The nailed marching boots of a Roman soldier.
Comitatus	The companions, or war band, of a chief or prince.
Loricae	The jointed shoulder guards of a Roman soldier.